**OVER
FOR
ROCKWELL**

OVER
FOR
ROCKWELL

Uzodinma Okehi

Short Flight / Long Drive Books
a division of HOBART

SHORT FLIGHT / LONG DRIVE BOOKS
a division of HOBART Publishing
PO Box 1658
Ann Arbor, MI 48106
www.hobartpulp.com/minibooks

Copyright © 2015 by Uzodinma Okehi

All rights reserved

ISBN: 978-0-9896950-4-6

Printed in the United States of America

Inside text set in Times
Cover art by Uzodinma Okehi

Rockwell/Contents

Black Million Dollar Man	1
What Else?!	5
Blue Curtain	6
Another Tragedy	7
Cubes	8
Repulse Bay	11
Sleep Tickles	14
Live to Relax!	43
Chasm!	44
Bollywood Starlet	45
Immortality is Yours!	46
Seven-Foot Tall Ballhandlers	49
Live to Relax! (part 2)	68
Thousand Shining Kindness	69
Sword of Doom	71
Vanessa	72
Constellate That!	74
This Godforsaken Ease	77
Live to Relax (part 3)	82

84	Theory of Perpetual Motion
87	Centipedes
89	No More Flared Jeans
94	Tomb of Kings
95	And yes, I know only Sikhs wear Turbans
96	Tomb of Kings 2: Gold-Bowelled Cities
98	Call My Bluff
114	Colostomy
126	Bill Bixby
128	Timpani Drum
129	Buck Rogers Ring Tone
132	Empathy/remix
133	More Nightmares
138	Over For Rockwell
143	Soothe as Excalibur
145	Unbelievable Worlds (ass is magical!)
148	Streets of Rage
158	Strange Hush
159	Go-Backology
160	Art is Life: Compression
165	China Dog Syndrome
173	The Guillotine

Hong Kong	175
Hide if You Have To	179
Hong Kong/1995	182
Technological Laser	183
Shazambro!	185
Tomb of Kings (part 3)	188
The Vegetal Kingdom	190
Get to the Chopper!	200
Butyrate Fuse	202
The Rub	205
Cats That Walk Through Walls	206
Entropy	209
Art is Life: Pursuance	211
Tumescent Guise	212
Life of Jo-Jo	218
No Chop	243
Hulk Intro Mix	244
Wendee	248
Sososososo . . .	251
Nothing Works	253
Thanh	263
The Suburbs	265
Two-Man Weave	266
Tostones	269

272 Satkhira
275 Canned (amazon book review)
278 Bela
279 Fortress (starring Christopher Lambert)
282 Jie, Lue
286 The Deuce
290 Monisha
296 Cumulo-Nimbus Tonight!
311 SupaMillenialNight-Speed Falcon
325 Space is the Place

Like a man cured of AIDs. Yeah, I feel free.
—Valdes
—2012 (via text message)

Black Million Dollar Man
(New York City 1999)

One of the big things I told my pals growing up in the suburbs, was about how I was gonna tame the city, make it my own. And not just drawing comics! *Man*, I was going to date models, starlets, heiresses . . . Because if the city was a jungle, they could believe me, those girls would just be there swinging, available fruit . . . But more than models, it was because a guy like me was born for cities, made to move, born to burst into flame at a moment's notice, to devour everything: ideas, girls, money, scenery, concepts, name it; the food on your plate, the air in your lungs and mine, not only that, I'd douse the light from the sky, I'd suck it all in like smoke and after that, I'd tear up big chunks of asphalt with my teeth . . . I'd make pendulums swing when I got there, not just the starlets . . . I'd bathe in fountains, cure banality, fake miracles and when all was said and done I'd be able to come up with something better than to just revisit the wrongs I felt had been done to me.

Jump cut from that to years later . . . From the suburbs to Iowa City, to Hong Kong, to Changking, the Wing Wah and back, then to New York, where after a year the only model I'd managed to meet was Teena; whose opinion of me varied, I'm sure, here to there, but really never got up much higher than, say, upper-middle, but friend-zone, since I was of little substance, I guess, and since, like me, she was always on the make, always trying, searching for something better and still scrambling just to survive. And as little as I had left to hope for then, there was still no better choice but to dive right into it. Dive down into nights like deep felt, strange hush, gliding through sheets of fog, and always bitter, freezing cold on those nights, pounding the sidewalks with my pal Valdes, with that inkling, as if the city had already failed me. Maybe I'd planned to be a billionaire, but by then I hardly remembered all I said I'd do. Or that night on Ludlow, right off Houston, I can still hear my footfalls in the snow, in place, pacing, from side to side. She never smoked, she'd said, but there was Teena, there with me, underneath the awning outside Max Fish, asking for a light. I'd been telling her that I was a complete failure. I was admitting that, but by now I'd come up with the knack to say it as if there was in fact no better way to live. We were huddled together against the side of the building, so close that I could see steam coming off the apples of her cheeks. An absolute failure—*that's the way one had to think about it*—up until this single, shining moment! So many things I'd dreamed of had proved to be just too big, too far out of reach. Just like those snowflakes, drifting in, melting, to teardrops against her forehead, down, across the bulb of her lips, like that, more than a million miles away! And yet I couldn't throw myself off a cliff, that's what I told her, that was my little song, but it was still the truth. There was still nothing else for me to do other than keep dreaming, keep barreling forward with even bolder, even more unlikely pipe-dream plans. I was already an adult, there was hardly a chance, and yet every day, in between naps, like a man barely alive, I was still trying to re-make myself bigger, cooler. Better . . .

What Else?!

They say it takes an average person about 10 years to master a given thing. This was my thinking in 1995 when I dropped out of college in Iowa City to draw comics. Because I'd seen a lot of movies, I figured Hong Kong was the place, so I went there, hoping to put a tap on that excitement. After that plan went bust I tried another, then another. I put down the pen too many times to count, only to pick up again because there was nothing else. If there was a theme to come away with it was that nothing is ever as easy or even as worthwhile as "They" make it seem. The years passed and I was just as deluded, but also still excited, about drawing, though my life was just as ordinary. My name is Blue Okoye. Anyway, that's the short version . . .

Blue Curtain

A box without hinges, key or lid— Like my room in Changking, Ching Wren's place was another prison in which the most I could ever seem to do was dream successfully. No door, just that blue curtain, printed with caricatures of Chinese children and which sighed throughout the day, rippling with sounds of feet and voices; with death, life, sorrow and excitement. I'd lie on the floor just listening, and in that sense it didn't seem so bad to be dreaming and not drawing, *all those thousands of lives*, to feel so content idling mine away . . .

Another Tragedy!

Heave over, huge void, a hole at the front of the page from which I'd burst into drawing non-sensical, squiggling lines. And no technique, what I wanted was for her to see me still fighting, sweating it out each night when she came home. Each evening I'd draw right through one page to the next, until the entire ream was a sea of sheets crumpled beneath the table. *Another tragedy!* That's what I wanted on the page, though back then I'd have been satisfied to give her some little picture of maybe a panda, or a schoolbus . . .

Cubes

Heave over, huge void, a hole at the front of the paper from which I burst into drawing nonsensical, squiggling lines, page after page. If no pages left then fill the spaces between the lines, verge toward black, then back to little cubes . . . All this to draw the school bus at the corner of the same city scene I've been struggling with, hacking and erasing, chipping away for months. I could start by drawing a bus, but I know better. I could refer back to the photo I took my first week in Hong Kong—that drizzling street-scape soaked with grey—to tell me all I ever need to remember about futility, about parables, like Sisyphus, about a kind of beauty that always seems just beyond reach.

The beauty of it is each evening when Ching Wren comes home, that shine of pomade in her eyebrows, and she piles a fresh ream of typing paper in front of me on the coffee table. The futility is the fine misunderstanding between us, rather, that miracle, but I tell myself I can't get too sidetracked wondering what she really thinks. Then about those cubes . . . I can try anything, draw any and everything to rev myself up, but I find I still have to come back to those cubes shooting through space, through contrails, leading back to pinpoints of perspective. These are the building blocks, the theory being that through drawing cubes, you can arrive at anything, mend any fence. Once, *just once*, I overturned that coffee table in a fit of rage, and even going over it felt wrong, there in her apartment, like some animal amok inside of a cathedral. That was the downside, when cubes fail and the new plan B is all those squiggling lines . . . *And Sakura, let me ease those lines into even avenues and breeze-swept city streets . . .* Each evening, and though I feel your eyes on my back I can't turn around, I won't utter a word, because I'm not just drawing again, I am that bus, silly as it sounds, and despite the mess in front of me, page after page, it's still those engines in my head, like: Voom! Voom!

Repulse Bay

Here we go, *another strange but true-told, Hong Kong myth*: I remember daybreak, waist-deep, standing fully clothed in the surf at Repulse Bay, holding an unopened bottle of vodka. It couldn't have been more than my second or third day off the plane, and maybe I'd expected it all to feel different, better somehow. I'd walked out of the hotel wearing brand-new pants, a leather jacket, and even at the time it was kind of funny, as if someone might toss over my shoulders a lei of pink flowers to complete the transformation . . . The myth was that you could escape your problems, when in fact there was nothing as mundane or more burdened than my same-old thoughts that night as I turned corners, drifted down walks and concrete flights, and by luck, somehow, I ended up on that beach. I never did open that bottle. Nor did I end up, quote-unquote, finding myself in Hong Kong, though that's probably what I was thinking when that sun came over the mountains, while I was spitting water, laughing in spite of myself with all that light there dazzling around me . . .

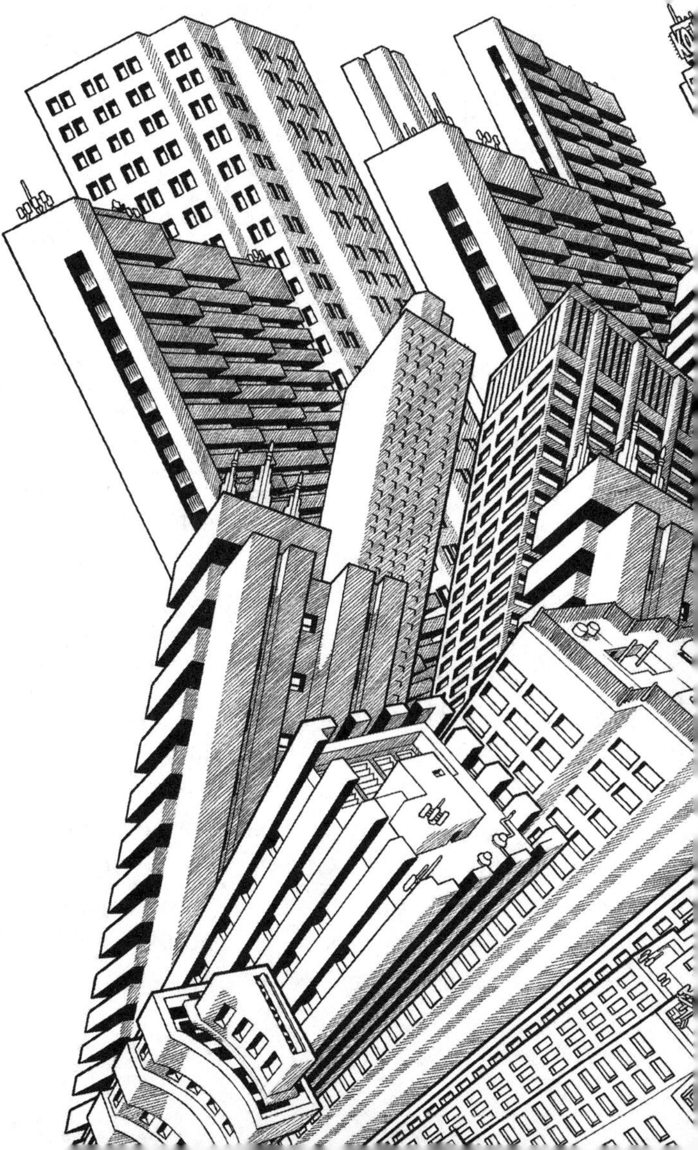

1: Sleep Tickles

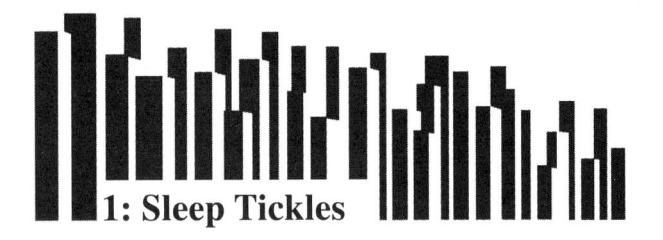

The delirium of those early nights, not at sea, but adrift in that chorus of giggling, laughing, widely smiling Chinese girls, that seething tableau of shining faces . . . This was Hong Kong, 1995, and that night I was lost as usual. Flailing. Stumbling drunk off a beer and a half, and with every conversation somehow spiraling quickly out of control. *Why did I sound so bitter?* That's what I asked myself, as the jokes all sputtered out unfunny and any backpedaling I tried just took me over the next ravine. Ching Wren was sandwiched in with the rest of those girls, her thin smile the one unmusical note as the others sighed and fluttered, cooed and snuggled, chortling like a flock of trained showbirds . . .

It was the Lost World club. My wingman was a Chinese pal of mine from college, but I'd already given up on that guy as an entrée to any sort of real excitement. The girls there were a crowd he'd known from high school, in sunglasses at 2am, cold magpies, over-dressed fashion plates, and so after about an hour we were both being roundly ignored. Other Chinese dudes were already stepping up, sidling down from the dancefloor and I guess I couldn't blame them. By then the talk had switched to Mandarin, or Cantonese, or whatever it was, effectively shutting me out, so I broke off to roam the place . . .

It could have been hours later, and I'd say I was stone sober by the time I kissed Ching Wren. I was down the hallway by the payphones, wide-awake, lying beneath a metal bench with my jacket balled up under my head . . . And this was already full-circle, after I'd been determined, felt defeated, then decided there was no choice but to stay loose, keep moving . . . From girl to girl . . . After bouncing, literally, with the music, through the club, room to room . . . Up to one of the waitresses, who made a point not to understand I was asking what time her shift ended . . . Incredulous, waving her hands: *"No, no* . . . Then, perched by a doorway that I later realized was the women's restroom, girls lined on either side, single file, one after another, brushing me aside . . . I tried to reset myself with a pull-up move at a table full of German girls . . . Just two guys, that's what I figured, girls to spare. *"Man, could I use a cigarette!"* I said, and why was I shouting? Then I tried to reset myself again, to back up and ask how they liked Hong Kong, but then that also sounded preposterous, moreso since I'd decided to say it with a "Charlie Chan" Chinese accent, that on top of the fact I'd also been there less than three weeks . . .

It was after all this when I was down under that bench, hands folded over my chest. First there'd been two pairs of feet, talking, walking up to use the phones, then giggling, trotting back . . . Then, with a lurch, someone sat down on the floor right next to me, and for a while there was only the sound of us both breathing . . .

The explanation I later gave, to Benoit, to everyone, was that I kissed Ching Wren, not because I was drunk but because that's the sort of thing you're supposed to do in life, to reach out, even if it makes no sense, even if you regret it afterwards. And after what seemed like decades, eons, there was a rustling sound, standing up, crouching down and then Ching Wren's face inches from mine, looking beneath the bench. All Chinese talk sounded like shouting to me, so she was there shouting, something like, "*you-go how!*" and I just leaned out and mashed my mouth against hers—not even a kiss—just our lips stunned open like fish puckering, and that half a second before she jumped up and padded off down the hall.

2: Sleep Tickles
(wobble-walk)

Meanwhile, how else to sum it up, how better, but with the one caveat that if I had things my way, I'd as soon stay asleep? The original plan had been to cut all ties, to leave school for a reason. But here I'd been in Hong Kong for almost four months, and while I'd barely drawn a stitch, I felt I'd beat those streets to death, feet to pavement, for weeks, months at a time with Benoit, chewing scenery, back and forth, chasing leads, roaming through nights or blazing over town like whirling platelets in the back of the red Hong Kong cabs . . . The idea had been to drop everything. I'd come to Hong Kong and I wouldn't budge until I'd made myself draw comics about it. Instead it was as if I was always somehow still back-to-back with Benoit, and I had to remind myself that we were hardly friends. With Benoit, flustered as usual, supreme torment, then cop-show cool, belting down drinks, circling his coaster with a fingertip, while on the other hand I had my doubts . . . With Benoit, for whom this thing with whores had become a relentless obsession! Or standing back, that was me, and with some measure of reserve, leaning against balustrades as he galloped about, sometimes shouting, sometimes accosting Chinese passersby in the street. Sometimes whispering: *Say buddy, yet lau, yet feng* . . . Or as he was always urging me, *just think about it! One room, one Phoenix* . . . It was the very fact that gems like this never seemed to elicit a response, not from Noi, not from any Chinese, that supposedly told us what we needed to know, that it was all right beyond our reach, fingertips against the glass in other words, and guys like us were meant to bust right through . . .

The ongoing mythology was that we were both excited about it, that for a while now we'd been convinced Benoit's Thai girlfriend, Noi, was a prostitute . . . And did it matter that Noi wasn't even Chinese? I asked myself because unlike Benoit I felt conflicted. The one thing I could say for myself was that I was no kind of sinophile, that none of it occurred to me clearly beforehand. But then there was Noi; easy, buttered thighs, no ass at all, but still with the tight shorts, and *yeah*, some kind of mystery . . . Wobble walk, too-high heels . . . The shine on her bare shoulders, leading me and Benoit down through night-lit doorways . . . Dancehalls and O-K karaoke rooms . . . And that mystery was miles-long, like the jet-black hair down her back. Like an undulating, billowing tide, sweeping us right through every myth or off-color joke we'd ever heard, every kung-fu comic, every bad movie, and all of that was still beneath the surface! I was often in the next room or right behind the wall with Benoit going full-tilt, whamming it into her like a hydraulic press. Or in the Kit-Kat lounge, trying not to seem like I was watching them maul all over each other . . . Meanwhile above ground, I was on the streets in an everyday deluge of people who seemed to look right through me. Benoit was rabid about it, but in my own way I was also head over heels, and *of course I came to Hong Kong to fuck Chinese girls!* I still thought a lot about drawing comics, but it was like one of those tiny islands, shrouded in haze, off the coast of Repulse bay. The nights were frantic, but they also seemed so much more alive, more real. I spent the bulk of my daylight hours exhausted, racked out on the dirty mattress in the room I'd rented in Changking. And even sound asleep, even in my dreams, there was the same debilitating lust like a sickness, a chronic fatigue, dampening everything, more and more, waking up, back to sleep, same cycle, and it was as if I could feel some vital part of myself draining away . . .

3: Sleep Tickles

And is it important for me to say who found who, later that night, in the crush of bodies outside the Lost World club? What I remember is, people looking, eyes riveted, following, and Ching Wren pressing against me as if it was just that we'd been unable to find each other all this time . . . From the beginning it was wordless, understood. It was also sloppy, almost futile, and no doubt we drew stares because there was no poetry in it. There, on the sidewalk, pawing under my jacket with alcohol steaming from her pores. Then on the road, veering, weaving through traffic, me on the back of her scooter, and instead of wearing the single helmet—because that was the way I felt—I let it hang from my fingers, dangling, now and then catching sparks from the road beneath us flying by . . .

And after those initial sparks, after the dead silence of what could have only been our second thoughts, after that we did manage to crash around half-clothed on the bed, but it didn't seem to make much sense . . . I struggled with then broke the clasp on her bra, and she knocked the wind out of me, putting a knee into my stomach as I kissed the ridge of bone at the center of her chest . . . And this was after floating, gliding up the stairs, no hesitation, after guiding me into her flat, holding two of my fingers in her fist . . . She rolled on top of me, breathing hard, but still wearing pants, still confused, maybe, and I guess I wasn't going to force it . . . This was after sitting on her bed, no time, just forever, eons, sitting bolt upright, the both of us, fully clothed and staring, as if she knew I was going to blink first . . .

My hands, rough, black stones, and just as clumsy, against the pale flesh of her back . . . Which was what I was telling myself even that first night: *We all find love then lose it* . . . Her place was a tenement room, sixteenth floor, the walls eggshell blue. The pairs of jelly sandals by the doorway, and one stray one. Stickers all over the side of the VCD stack . . . Ching Wren could have been the love of my life, but even so close, even on that bed, mouth to mouth, and I still couldn't seem to cross that gulf . . .

For what it's worth, and for whatever reason, I still think about it as much if not more than back then . . . The truth was I didn't know what to do so I just let the days go by. . . I should have walked out after that first night, probably, but I stayed there for more than a week, during which we rarely spoke even a few words . . . Thinking about it now, it's easy to maybe make too much out of it, but there was a kind of language between us. . . Sitting on the floor, wide-eyed, a couple of mimes, watching each other and grinning from opposite sides of that tiny room . . . Or while she was cooking, while I was on the bed sprawled out and sweating, or when I could smell the rain outside and she'd be right there tugging on my shirt . . . What else?! Her huge, silver-dollar nipples . . . scrubbing my hands through the forebrush bristles of her short haircut . . . That is to say, plenty of Tarzan/Jane moments, and I guess I was relieved it felt like love because all that big lust was gone . . .

But it was a lost cause, maybe that's what I felt we were grinning about! Like that first night with nothing accomplished, no way, no how, and bone tired, *bottle-pop*, when she pulled my finger out and held it to her chest and that's how I drifted off, falling, diving to sleep . . .

4: Sleep Tickles

And I'm telling you, she was about to slip. She was gonna blurt everything, I could feel it. I was sitting just like I am now. You know, legs crossed at the ankle, not too much, medium smirk. I was drinking coffee, just watching her. I was holding back, that's what I'm saying. And that's the part that kills me. I know that bitch! She's dying to tell me! She just can't bring herself to spit it out! Actually that's the part that excites me. I can admit it. Like everywhere else, the women here are inveterate liars. But here it's like they won't let up! No matter what, the charade must go on! Listen, by the time I'm done here, I'll tell you, I'm gonna write the damn book on these sluts! I was sitting there—whatever—nodding, small-talk, and like an epiphany, it was as if she could suddenly see the irony, she could see me steeped in it, Buddha-style, and that I could go on smirking for a thousand years if need be, spending money, fucking the shit out of her, and still never doubting it for a second! After all, what do we know about real girls? That's why it was there on the tip of her tongue. Guys like us, we have an instinct with whores because it's a symbiosis. They need us like we need them, and that's the part she couldn't admit. So instead, at the last minute, it's some lame bit about how she's had another boyfriend all this while. That she feels terrible for lying to me. And I suppose I'm playing for headway, but in my mind I'm like: Oh come on! A boyfriend! Try twenty, you bitch! Fifty! And that's even beside the point!

I was down on the mattress, eating cold noodles, watching Malaysian Strike Force on the VCD . . . Like with Benoit rambling, I was only halfway into it, halfway listening, because it was a scene I'd been through dozens of times . . . The big showdown. The main cop vs. the Japanese bad guy. They were wearing hyperbaric suits, facing off in an air-sealed chamber flooding with poisonous gas . . . As with most Chinese action pics, there was a lot of eye-popping wirework involved, some hair-raising near-misses with those little combat knives . . . Meanwhile, Benoit had worked himself into a lather. He'd leapt out of the chair and begun to pace around the room. He was spastic, muttering to himself, thumbing through my sketchbook, through my paperbacks and comics littered on the desk, quickly tossing them aside . . .

You know, and that's the irony! Tell one of these hoes you're in love and she wants to laugh in your face. On the other hand, whenever she deigns to say it, you feel forced to take it seriously in spite of yourself. No, the irony is that even here, all these girls willing to go at the drop of a hat, at the slightest whiff of a dollar, and yet still, secretly, pretending to themselves that it's some sort of spiritual journey. And don't act like you can't see what I'm talking about either. You can't name it any more than I can, but you can feel that Shangri-la, that something out there and it's the same reason all these chicks can't satisfy themselves working as waitresses. And you'd be in a better position to help me play this thing out if you weren't still stuck on what's-her-name . . . I mean how long are you going to stay cooped up here as if it's the end of the world? Listen, give me one way that she was any different from the rest and I'll leave you alone about it. Just one—but you can't! So what's holding you back? The memory of what could have been? Look, didn't you say that bitch could barely speak a word of English! Come on, what were you going to do, learn Chinese? What, settle down? Meet her family? Yeah, you're laughing, because it sounds just as bad to you! Which is exactly what I'm saying, pal, fuck that shit!

5: Sleep Tickles

Then later still, same cycle . . . Back to sleep, then wide awake, and I sat bolt upright from the mattress on the floor. I had no clock, no way of telling night from day, but because there was no excuse left, I started drawing . . . Pen to paper, page sideways, tracing a long curve—*deep breath*—and every mark I made somehow seemed to drift. I stopped. I got up and paced, I circled my spot in the corner a few times, then dove back into it . . . *Because like jumpshots, drawn lines fall and miss* . . . And that was my own voice, the little poems I repeated to myself, gritting my teeth, with sweat bursting through pores on my forehead. . . *Brick, bounce, slip and bank home*—then my pen skipped. I threw it across the room and took another. It wasn't just those girls dancing behind my eyes either. Also that cloudy mess on the paper in front of me, same struggle, the same uphill battle! Then on the other hand was the truth I was actually trying to draw, which I knew meant nothing to anyone, but still so clear, so futile now, and on the page so distant that the act of drawing was like trying to forget.

Benoit was always dropping by, that was the thing and that was always how it started. I'd be in that filthy room, no windows, the walls starting to dome in on me, my heart palpitating but with the magic seeping back into my fingertips . . . I'd be there, pencil in hand, poised over the drawing board when all of a sudden it was Benoit, thooming at the door as if there was an army at his heels. The ludicrous part about it was that we both thought of ourselves as great somethings—as artists—as if all it took was idle curiosity to change one's life. I was worse off than Benoit, in that I felt overwhelmed most of the time and I could never quite settle on what was driving me. Who was Ching Wren? Why did it matter? Who were all these other strobe-lit, invincible Chinese girls we imagined milling around underground, or down on empty dance floors waiting for us? Two douchebags, and yet this was the feeling, the euphoria that carried us out. And that was how we hit the streets, night after night; jogging in matched steps past the old Chinaman with his wooden cart, the benches in the courtyard, past the stone Buddha and out with a flourish onto the sidewalk to a soundtrack of trilled saxophones.

That particular night I'd just woken up when Benoit came crashing in, slamming the door shut . . . Then, again later, in the dead hours, beating with his fists, shouting at me through the door because I'd remembered to throw the bolt:

"HER HANDSOME AMERICAN FRIENDS! That's what they said, pal, and that's us! C'mon, I can hear you breathing! Blue! Blue, pal, get up! We've gotta get down there! Blue! Listen! This is no time to start acting funny . . .

Instead I drew until the walls of Jericho seemed to crash down around me, until my hands trembled and I could no longer think. Then I pushed the drawing board aside and moved about the room in a daze. I gulped the strains from a half-crushed can of soda. I turned on Malasian Strike Force, then clicked it off again. By now Benoit was on some couch somewhere smothered in ass, and the fact that this, what I was doing, seemed like the high road was no great relief. But Benoit wasn't the problem . . . I felt like screaming, breaking something, but instead I unclipped my drawing book from the board, flung open the door and stormed into the hallway. That soft, tropical sigh of rain on the roof, down the walls in pipes. Same cycle, same lump in my throat. And after a few tries I was able to snap free the rusted latch and hurl the book down through the open window.

6: Sleep Tickles

It didn't even make sense. Just the same, I felt I owed that Chinaman an explanation . . . Him and his wooden cart, like a miniature temple on wheels, intricately carved with script in bas-relief, and with no other obvious function than to provide a place for him to crawl into and sleep there on the breezeway. So far, it was this old man who had been my inscrutable orient, my conscience, maybe, my svengali, as well as an unblinking sentinel to all those limitless nights. *For instance:* That morning I finally picked up and left Ching Wren's place, after all the silence had bled into too many doubts and there was nothing left but to give up, to let go, slip out while she slept, to stumble all night through the streets until I found my way back to Changking mansions with dawn spilling into the courtyard . . . There as always, it was the old man, not waiting, just watching, arms at ease, perched on his little stool. That morning, the same as the many times afterward when I'd have given anything for some sane word of reproach! I'd tell him that it was as if I'd been using her, I felt that way about it, only I couldn't figure out exactly how. Then again, where was the whimsy, the sage-like smirk and knowing cadence leading into little word-poems about rustling leaves assuaging guilt? Now more than ever, when I could've used a Chinese sage, here was this guy, still mute, and looking pretty satisfied with himself . . . And how many nights, in the throes of that guilt, had I thrown myself down to sit across from him on the concrete—*hoping for what*, to go back in time? I'd tell him, if I could, that it wasn't until months later I found out from my Chinese pal that her name was actually *Chien Lien*, and that I'd burst out laughing because it was like the emblem of how much I'd been wrong about everything. Maybe if I could get him to laugh too, or to cringe, thinking about me and Ching Wren hugging and mooning over each other, maybe then I could wash it out of my system. Or at least this was what I'd think to myself sitting across from him. While he was a rock, perched in boxer shorts, nodding occasionally, as he always did, smoking his pipe . . .

 I was down in the chute, the narrow chasm made where the inside facing walls from the three towers of Changking Mansions almost touched. It was still night, still wet, as I plowed around and climbed through that ocean of stinking plastic sacks. The rain was soaking my A-shirt, running down my face in rivulets. The mound of garbage was almost seven feet, some in bags, some loose, spilling from dumpsters, riding along the walls like ivy. I cut a mean swath, throwing aside bundles and rotting clumps as I made my way toward the center, because it had to be there somewhere on top . . . And because I'd lost count, *I don't know, couple times*, I wondered how many nights had that old man seen my sketchbook come flying from the window on the eleventh floor, down into the chute, then hours later watched me go tearing up that mountain of garbage like a man on fire? I could feel him watching me, his eyes on my back as I found it mashed in with a sopping wad of newspapers, still half dry. The truth was that sketchbook was full of nothing but failure, and maybe that's what I wanted to hear, that every mistake has meaning. He could have told me anything, in English or otherwise, I'd tack on the divine part, but he just stood down there on the ramp, unblinking as always and with his hands clasped, as if it was the closing seconds of some rousing event. Still no smile, no nothing, still nodding, but because it seemed like he was expecting something big I held up the book . . .

"Old man." I said, *"What else is there?"*

Live To Relax!

My tack was to bury myself, to play video games, order pizza, read the tabloids, to sleep for days. Like anyone, I could often feel regret seeping in, and while I'd admit it was no remedy, there was some real solace in those hours, decades, that I must have spent dozing on the couch . . .

Chasm!

Which is what I thought to myself time and time again, shrugging upstream on crowded streets or perched on stoops in the embers of evening light—that maybe there was no end to it! Maybe there was no final thing to look forward to, no great epiphany or single happiness that could make all the scrambling you had to do in the end seem worthwhile. Then also was my portfolio, like a ton of bricks slung across my back. What I wanted from life was just to relax, and yet I thought so much about comics, about art back then, that it became just like money or sex, just another long vault on the way down that bottomless chasm!

Bollywood Starlet
(*Sorry Teena!)

Teena was too fine to draw*, Bollywood starlet, and of course that meant she was destined for something. There were also the times I'd try to think in her shoes, but it made the world seem just too crazy, too evil, I'd say, to have everyone always leering at me, smiling in my face . . .

Immortality is yours!

Crack! That was the sound of our hearts stopped, the crunch of my soles against the pavement, and I pushed off, straight up from the curb, a thousand feet into the air . . . And what can you ever really do given the situation? Even had any of us been able to act, to move, what was there to say? Because time never slows, in fact those are the moments where your mind moves like the hummingbird; touching, dancing over each little thing, or floating, time as an ocean, and that break-beat is wave upon wave of perspective. Could I have known, for instance, as we watched that girl crossing the street in front of us, that one day, years later, Valdes would stand-up at his office job, tear off his tie and begin screaming at the top of his lungs? Or that Goezman would end up in the penthouse of an apartment block, living with two women as a kind of pasha, a slumlord, that he would also be dead before his thirty-fifth birthday? How many times between now and then would I say I'd stopped stock-still to watch some girl's ass from behind? Ass from the future. Ass encompassing everything, like two snow-capped mountains crashing together. And not to dwell on it too much, but I felt ashamed to be there frozen. All I could think that night was about the plot of the shitty movie we'd just seen, about the Trojan war, with that white hero killing everybody, giving those speeches about immortality and whatnot. And who's to say those moments *don't* last forever, that somewhere behind us we're not still making the same mistakes, taking the same wrong forks in the road, overestimating ourselves again and again?

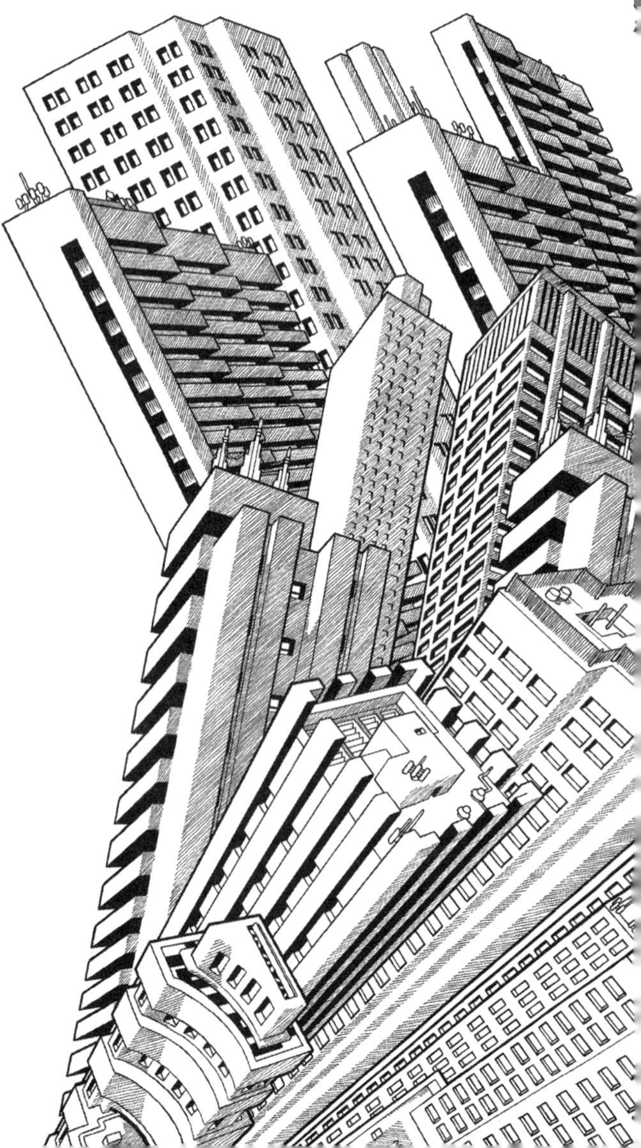

1: Seven-Foot Tall Ballhandlers
(New York City 2002)

And what else is there beside the fact of the clock always moving, albeit imperceptibly, tiny ticks? Teena-baby, each of us, we react, move or don't move and what I think is, it's pure guts that puts us on the side of the angels. In other words, there is no destiny, there are no greater truths. I don't mean to talk as if I know all there is to know, so instead I'll confess I've never been a winner, but I need the exercise, and I've always gotta sweat, talking to you. Which I guess is what I'm getting at with this business about seven-foot tall ballhandlers . . .

I was saying that; nervous, coughing it up in chunks, but I remember also thinking that every guy, sooner or later, is gonna get caught on a girl like Teena. This was years back, and if you follow basketball it was one of those seasons with the T-wolves where Kevin Garnett was unstoppable, sweating it out every night like a man possessed. And by the way, Teena was the type to smile, full-on, when she saw you. A girl that smooth, that wide smile, in and of itself a stumbling block, was also a kind of unusual generosity. But then again, it wasn't just me; guys were all about Teena, the lane clogged with traffic. I was watching a lot of sports that summer, maybe because I was also big trophy hunting, which turned out to involve a lot more waiting than anything else. Sitting around scheming, biding my time. After all, you can call the same few girls—even Teena—only so much. And of course it was formulaic! I guess I felt torn about it. I was in every way a flake, a phony.

I was relentless, also a fighter. I was hungry, like kids from those commercials who live off a dollar a day, but sympathy wasn't enough. I'd be in the cubicle at work, or on breaks outside at the pay phone. I'd call girls one after another, down the list, like applying for jobs, like playing roulette. Like lottery tickets. *This one's my number—or not*, that's what you told yourself, because one way or another it was a game you had to play. Because game or no game, you were still out there flailing, struggling. Details didn't matter because there were always far too many of them; too many issues, too many long distance boyfriends and blind dates gone wrong, too many theories and friends with privileges, and all that really mattered was being out there, on the court, that it was me and some girl, Teena maybe, *lucky night*, but it was still only instinct, only human for me to try and beat the buzzer with a miracle shot. It was formulaic but then so was the every-game sight of KG doused in sweat, crossover dribble, in off the right wing, in art as in life, two steps, beeline for the hole.

2: Seven Foot-Tall Ballhandlers

There's the point after which, I think, a certain grade of bullshit can transcend the truth. You strain hard enough, you bewilder yourself, and even the most superficial moments can seem to shine. That was the idea, and it was what I told Teena while we were out there shining, night after night: *You keep on shooting, no matter what. Not only that, you gotta try and dig deeper* . . . And after a while there was nothing but the idea itself, extrapolated, the furthest extent. It became my one-note theme, but also a symphony, a masterpiece. Pump-faking jumpshots with my crumpled falafel bag, at 2am outside St. Marks church. Drink-cans, with snack wrappers. That is, jab-stepping, lunging, arcing up 20-foot rainbows into trash cans inside art galleries, delis, movie theatres, East Village dive bars. Which was what it turned into from the first night, out with Teena, after waiting more than a week for her to call, so many things I'd planned to say, other topics, then somehow I locked onto the basketball thing and ran with it.

By day I was about to lose my job. I was losing weight, barely sleeping. In theory I'd have used the time to draw comics, since that was my thing. Instead I was watching Sportscenter, the NBA channel, highlight reels. I'd never been so riveted to sports before, but there I was, and I needed that juice to hit the streets again with Teena.

Like that very first night . . . The night after that night; in my apartment, pacing, trying not to think about it too much, clenching my fists, reliving the little scene where she'd written her number on my arm at the party, TV blaring, I was crumpling up sheets of tinfoil to practice KG's headfake and turn-around dropstep in my kitchenette. But back to that first night. *Should I feel lucky or sad about it, Teena, you tell me . . .* Low lights and music. Booze in plastic cups. Another Brooklyn house party. Another round of me with my cigarette, back against the wall, in there looking bored, the same as everyone else. Maybe Teena was different because it seemed even before I started talking as if she'd been waiting for someone to come over, to come up with something, anything. Maybe it was that overall generosity. I could say that Teena was the type of fine that meant she was destined for something. I could talk about her face, Bollywood starlet, that smile, about the little pouch of her stomach as we stood there talking about nothing, but then again maybe the most important thing was the moment before that, the gut-prick, gnawing agony, watching her dance a step aside from her friends, in that aqua dress and slowly, holding her drink, not bouncing, but dropping, twisting in the baseline, and no our eyes didn't meet, I just decided I'd seen enough. I put down my cup and pushed off from the wall.

3: Seven Foot-Tall Ballhandlers

I never laid a finger on Teena. I wasn't able to, and maybe that's the part to admit. Maybe the chance wasn't there or maybe when it came to the moment I couldn't force myself. The last time I saw Teena was eight or nine years after, on the subway, and it seemed somehow cruel for her to barely recognize me, that she couldn't remember my name. Then again, the thing with Teena had ended the way these "things" usually do; that is, softly, vaguely crumbling, as barely a thing at all, as the dust that gathers between better stories, swept underfoot . . . And maybe the sports metaphor is too cheap for her, like my stained polo shirts and torn jacket. I want to be honest about it, I want to live out my delusions in the open, and that was me and Teena, that night after we'd walked all up and around First Avenue with linked arms, then down, stretched out on that bench, looking up at the lights atop the buildings like stars. Those endless roundabout tours of the East Village. It's the very fact you've exchanged and heard all the same stories before that frees you, allows you to get cozy, to be spellbound. Aside from Teena, even with the rejection, all the cold calls and freeze-outs I was still able to get a girl every now and then, but that's not the point. The secret, if there is one, is that it's a numbers game, about repetition, and you survive the heartbreak by staying loose, not angry. In that sense the basketball bit was like an epiphany, the same old song, but also the only thing I could think of that was even close to the truth. It was always a moment of sudden resolve, coming up with another little basketball spiel. I thought that if I could show her what it really felt like, talking to her, striving for it, if I could put her in my shoes for even a moment then it might make all the difference. I told her that there was something special, almost dangerous about being so nimble at seven feet . . . *Teena, think about it; the agony, the triumph* . . . That kind of skill was superb, yet costly . . . *If you watch someone that tall dribbling, it's as if every move, every drive to the hole is twice as strenuous as it would be for someone half the size. My theory is that it has to do with heavier bones, which sounds funny, I know. But if you really think about the skeleton of someone seven feet tall, those femur bones by themselves have to weigh nine or ten pounds each. Now picture those things swinging around like pendulums in a drive to the hoop. You watch it on TV, you see those guys sweating rivulets and you don't even realize what you're seeing is like a miracle. . .*

4: Seven Foot-Tall Ballhandlers

Teena telling me about the Jersey shore, about growing up. And I remember it sounding like my own life, anyone's, or not anyone, but to look at Teena you don't expect that snapshot of isolation, blurred around the edges; the boardwalk, overcast skies, the calliope music in the background.

But that was me and Teena, special moments—*your childhood and mine*, and strolling around, until, like that, it was all over. In retrospect, I'm sure there was some hallmark after which she got sick of me talking about basketball. Another note, speaking of calliope music, I'd never been fired from a job, and I held the streak by arriving to work on a Tuesday, looking around, then on impulse deciding to quit, because it seemed inevitable, only to be told with some relief they'd planned to fire me by the end of the week . . .

Or *what about before Jersey? Born in Danville, California, her father was white. Teena Shah. Five foot Ten. Her mother's surname, divorced. The year she'd spent modeling in Europe, and she could admit her head wasn't in it. In Milan she once blew six thousand dollars on porcelain dolls.*

What about the punk phase, spiked belts and jean vests, up and down the Lower East Side, because the suburbs in Jersey seemed so stifling. What else? Older boyfriend, the "six years" she refers to cryptically, the tattoo of a rose she later had burnt off with a laser.

That summer, post-Teena, post employment and I was rudderless, drifting. Kevin Garnett and the Timberwolves were exed out early in the playoffs, opening round. I was back to drawing comics, struggling, the usual lackluster results. Despite everything I felt upbeat, though I couldn't explain it at the time.

Those pseudo-beatnik, neo-punk dog days. Her head wasn't all there either, what with summers in Spain, Kathak dance classes, and meanwhile she was also flying through college with straight A's, coming home at night to read while her friends stayed out and overdosed, in St. Marks and Tompkins Square.

Until, finally, her Blue period. Get it? She'd punch me in the arm, but also laugh loudly, stupid joke . . . If just being with Teena was time running out, you could say I got caught watching the clock and the moment slipped through my fingers. I was dejected, but mainly exhausted, confused. All of a sudden it seemed ludicrous to sit around watching professional sports in my underwear. Nor did it seem sane anymore to spend five nights a week trawling for girls. What I later heard was she'd had an on and off boyfriend, Chilean, or from Spain, or something, and she'd flown out to see him. Looking back, I suppose there was the looming notion of some other guy. A feeling, maybe. But then again, given the scheme of how things turned out, *I* was more likely that lurking figure, the fleeting notion, which would probably have made the most sense.

5: Seven Foot-Tall Ballhandlers

What else? I could tell you about the end of that summer into fall, then February, getting my first job in a bookstore, a new era, but that's neither here nor there. It was during this period I'd wake up in the afternoon, still jobless, I'd buy coffee, a newspaper, I'd get on the subway, any train, and ride to the end of the line. Then back. Which is a thing most people don't believe about the city until they've lived here. That sooner or later, actually, again and again, like it or not, you're bound to cross paths with almost everyone you know and probably on the subway. Whether you make eye contact or not, whether you say something. Whether you think it's too soon or too late. Out of eight million people, and it wasn't the last I saw of Teena, just the time I think I handled it right . . . I was on the 3 train, heading home. The car was packed with a crush of Filipino women who'd seemed to explode in all directions; barking, crinkling shopping bags, ice in oversize drinks, the swish-swipe of tight jeans and shifting buttocks. All that chattering. I was unnerved, for whatever reason, and I failed to notice Teena for two or three more stops. I looked up and she was there, watching me evenly, uncrossing her arms over a sweater the color of butter. We held a steady gaze for minutes, swaying with the trundling of the car, and the cloud of noise made it convenient since there was nothing to say. At the 28th street stop she paused, for some reason measuring the seconds with great deliberation, before stepping off onto the platform, before turning to break into a smile in front of the window. Which, when I thought about it later was pound for pound, in that as much as all the BS I'd concocted to say to her, this too was a kind of riddle without any real meaning. A bizarrely chimeric, truthful smile, apples in the cheeks, a smile too wide for you to completely believe. The train picked up speed through the tunnel. I was also by then grinning big. And those Filipino chicks, whatever they were chattering about, they were smiling too.

Or what about those long, long baseline jumpers, Teena, on that little hoop they used to have at the Toys R' US on 45th street? And that's after strolling around, talking, after spending all day in that huge store roaming like children. In some ways it's the fact we all inevitably have to think about fucking that spoils it, which was I why I was glad for that hoop, to have that metaphor, which I'm sure was in that smile of yours that made my heart curl into a fist, why you tossed me that foam-covered ball and bet I couldn't hit them over that swarm of kids from the top of the aisle . . .

Live to Relax!
(part 2)

Maybe I'd told Teena so many times that I convinced myself! Over and over on the phone, or as we strolled the East Village, I depicted myself to her as a kind of great civil rights hero. She could laugh, but the way I chose to combat the evils of the world was by being just sincere and deliberate about everything I did. Maybe the clarity of this was easy to overlook, given that I spent most of my time sleeping, and of course it was a ploy to get her into the sack. On the other hand, I thought: *what if, w*hat kind of world could it really be if in fact the ideal was to live to relax?

Thousand Shining Kindness

The secret of ants and bees, of civilization, is that at any given time no one individually seems to have much of a clue. And like that, there was a certain point after which I began to nakedly observe this idea in motion, for instance, in the countless bookstore gigs that seemed to be the only kind of job I could ever stand. Maybe it was different in bookstores, and I suppose there was always that part of me just being lazy. I'd take my cup of coffee and when the mood struck me I'd be gliding around, smirking and talking to people, or just cruising by watching the obvious schemes built up over the years to make it look as if we were always working at a breakneck pace . . . One way to put it would be to say, about a certain bracket of society, that the average work day all over the world was usually spent doing next to nothing. I chose to tell myself that this was no scheme, but in fact the glue that held cities together, like unsaid thoughts talking, brick to brick.

Sword of Doom

Time speed-up, *stumblefoot*, seems like three days total in a summer month. One thing about life as a failure is I never get bored anymore, nor do I ever have enough time to sleep. Sex drives some people, or money, or those that believe in art as some divine form of revenge. And maybe so. What I think about is my last big fuck-up, this week's stumble, whatever it was, and after a while drawing comics is the easiest part. I want to make new memories, better ones, instead of wincing, and there's still time left . . .

Vanessa

I suppose I was always at a loss as to what I could say or do about it. My own best gestures never felt real to her and aside from that I could never seem to find the words. *That's it?* She'd say, and maybe she was right . . . But yeah, the whole thing was like an underwater struggle. I say that now, having had years to think about it. Every day, it was a wrestling match against an unimaginable leviathan, with both of us, me and her, on either side, pulling and huffing. Sometimes we were pulling apart, but sometimes I'd swear that we really wanted to be together, though either way it came out predictably the same. The same whipping, lashing momentum, punctuated by vicious strikes. Same cold vacuum, those silences, same undertow, in which both of us, most of the time, found it impossible to breathe . . .

Constellate That!

And not just those cringeworthy moments you carry around—for what—ten, twenty years? Those times you meant to apologize but somehow got lost, stalled, you couldn't . . . All those eclipsed moons, those quick comebacks strangled in your throat, or like that time with Aidele Cooper on the back of your Kawasaki bike, and you kept picturing the both of you crashed, screaming, broken against the asphalt. Like Kate Simmons in her pink jean jacket, sitting on that low wall, the ocean behind her, and it was before you knew what that meant. Not any one thing, but those moments together, big bolus, pick it apart, *man*, con-stellate that . . . No bones about it, no retribution, no real clean-up, just day after day, just days when you recoil, when you wince at all the ordinary life that you've wrought. But even after you've declared yourself a failure you still have to move, to go from there. Or you can wait it out, *just sit,* stare at the drawing board, your hands trembling. Or remember what your pal Valdes once told you, remember that, not the scene, just the words, *that the only real genius is action.*

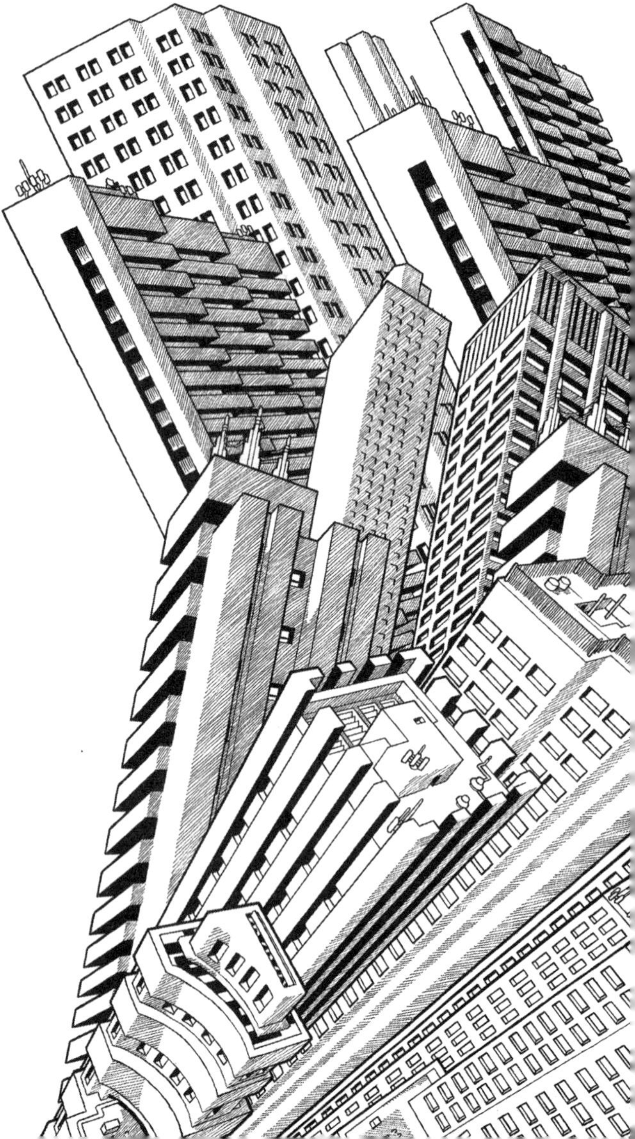

This Godforsaken Ease
(New York City 2003)

Like day to night, from waylaid, futile days, like wasted light, to nights like the pad of my feet down cobbled walks, on streets the names of which I still can't remember . . . Like dead afternoons, dissolved to fruitless nights, where I must have covered the entire city—which was what it felt like—top to bottom, just walking, a half-empty carton of orange juice dangling from my thumb and middle finger . . . Compare that to being buffeted, thrown and jostled, up at 6am sharp in streets awash with desperate faces, same as mine, to clangorous, outlandish city days exculpated from all rhyme or reason . . . Or something like that . . .

But also all around me and as always, it was still the same tune, like: *Hustle, hustle, do this, buy that, believe the tabloids, catch the award shows* . . . And I wouldn't wonder about it, but that was also what I'd come here to do, to hustle . . . Then again, I was also sweating bullets trying not to think about my rent, two months past due . . . About that tooth I could feel on the left side, hollowing out, like a three hundred dollar itch . . . Or that my clothes were almost tattered . . . Meanwhile out on the streets, with all the other hustlers, it was as if I was also always wading through crowds of fine, fine girls, all sneering at my clothes and my rail-thin physique . . . That is, finer than my own girl then, Vanessa, that spray of pimples across the bridge of her nose, and she was the one after me all the time to try and look better, fuck better, to exfoliate, to meditate on this and that and eat only fresh fruits, guavas . . . She could draw better than me too, I could admit that was a sticking point, but she'd already begun to realize that I was just another soft douchebag, no hustle, and it was only a matter of time before like Hayao Miyazaki, she felt the pull, before she was spirited away . . .

But even I was fed up with myself . . . Sick to my guts! . . . I'd ride on the subway for hours, back and forth, and like the world through the windows passing me by, it was hard to stop thinking about the ice-white smiles of the celebrities in those tabloids . . . I felt as if I'd been somehow made drunk by all this unrelenting hustle, sucked into it, when in fact my own picture of myself was less like a striver, and more like a kind of cartoon cherub with that same smile . . . Compare that to my very first sit-down, over drinks, with a so-called big-time comics editor, where after only a single beer nothing

I said seemed to stick, and to clean it up I kept having to go too-too deep, with too many weird pronouncements, until it was all smiles all around and finally things had digressed too far . . . Just hours before I'd been thinking this was gonna be it, my big break, but here I was with my script face down on the table, with my portfolio zipped at my feet, talking to this balding, genial motherfucker, about the war in Iraq, about how there was just something about Chinese girls, *yeah*—(what?)—about the best kind of, goddamn, frappuccino coffee and how he'd been a narcoleptic since age fourteen . . . And like a whirlwind, I then found myself right back on the streets, my hands shaking, groping for answers, asking myself what came before all the delusion, the daydreams and formulas on how to live one's life that had me sweltering, cracking under the strain, as if somehow waiting for permission . . .

Or, third-type, like those livid nights, in bed while Vanessa slept, staring at the ceiling, and then, like a mantra, each morning, thinking to myself: *I've just got to find my way back.*

Live to Relax!
(part 3)

Give me that gift Sakura, where there's no solace in life. Lift me from my troubles . . . Rather, what I mean is to talk about the chorus of angels that I could always seem to hear right outside the door, or through the window whenever I was drawing. Often it was an actual party, or just people outside, laughing, mingling. Other times it was the huge celebration I imagined went on without me, a procession with elephants and roasting spits, sitars and costumed dancers repeating with their feet the thunder of drums. Maybe it was just too far-fetched to pit myself against the world, and I guess I would have been out there dancing with everyone else if it was ever that easy. I can remember being ten or eleven years old, trying too hard for dances with girls—something not right about it—and maybe that's how I ended up drawing comics. Where is it that we get this idea that one's life can ever really be wasted? Moreso than dancing, I can tell you about that great welling within me, not doing, just looking at pictures, of dances, celebrations in foreign streets, of people herding through shopping malls or calmly loitering as if that emptiness was the only mystery left. But Sakura, I told myself I had to keep going, I had to draw comics, for one, because of those dreams I've always had where I'm out on that crowded sidewalk and I'm finally able to stretch out with my eyes closed on the concrete, and because I think I know the end, that embrace, as they say, is like going into a deep, deep sleep . . .

Theory of Perpetual Motion

She was getting a poo-belly from drawing all the time, a little mound of fat that wattled, that danced and blurped around as she worked, drawing comics with her half-panicked, haphazard verve. She never quite kicked back the chair, but then sometimes she'd go for hours without sitting, hovering, that little squat, crouching, tensed over the table, flying across those pages with the brush . . . Vanessa . . . And I was always questioning—or trying to— the fact that she had no life anymore, apart from her gung-ho indie comics friends, and when was the next convention, *or what kinds of fucking nibs have you been using*, and talking about Star Wars, and so on. Maybe what I questioned was my own place in all of it. At the time I was doing more thinking than drawing, going around Brooklyn in the middle of the night feeling stultified, in Park Slope, in Flatbush—I'd walk around until I was good and worked up, then back to her apartment, I'd pull her down from the table, get her up against the wall on the futon and whale away. I'd watch her tits and that weird little belly splashing around until I felt disgusted. And I suppose there must have been some resentment. Why else, lying in the dark, would those conversations seem so much like indictments, like she was nagging me about it:

"Ok. Fine. But, no, think about how that sounds. Like imagine if I were to say it. I don't have time and all, so I'm going to give up doing comics. Meanwhile I'm gonna keep watching sitcoms every night. I'm gonna play video games and go to parties with

Valdes. I mean, Blue, you can do whatever you want. I'm just saying. Sounds stupid."

Centipedes

Man, that glad-act, all that drink-fueled shucking and smiling! It was all fake, a kind of necessary evil, but there was a tipping point, after which neither of us could stand it anymore. Often it wasn't even when those nights wound down, but like a switch within the both of us, after which we'd fold up and leave the party without so much as a parting word. And after so many nights that frustration was palpable, so much so—even surrounded by girls— that I'd look up on cue at Valdes, his hand in the air, and it was a kind of telepathy in the way we wrapped it clean with that single, orchestrated chop . . .

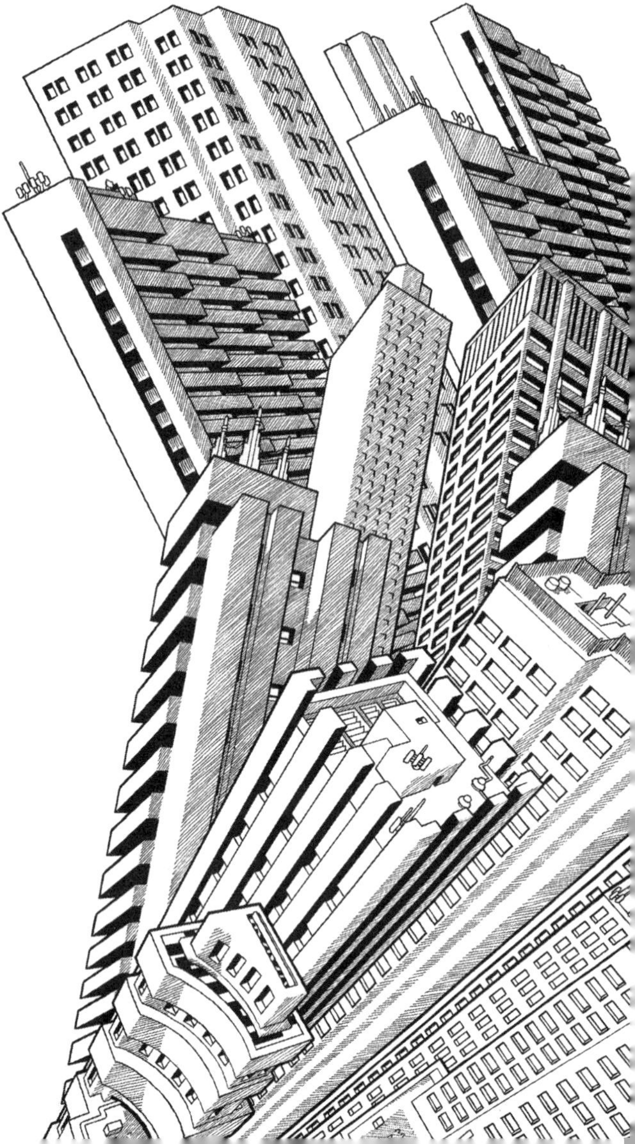

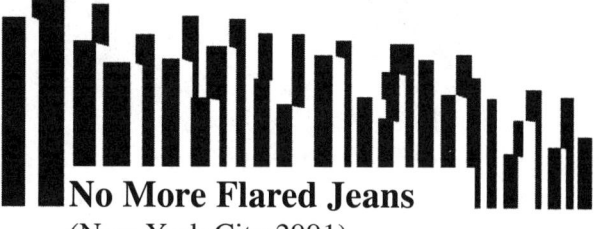

No More Flared Jeans
(New York City 2001)

Between you and me though, maybe it's that we choose our own lot . . . Maybe what I mean is that with art you can pretend it makes you free, you can go whichever way you want with it, but just maybe the first thing you always have to learn is how to bounce, how to go the hard way down through that chasm, that great multitude of things one can't and shouldn't do . . . That is, *Chasm*, as in New York City, as in the all-too true fact that everyone seemed to have a manuscript, a portfolio or something wistfully artistic in hand . . . As in, you gotta feel it for yourself, that sheer weight of so many forlorn hopes . . . *Chasm,* as in graduate school, where I could barely stay awake during the lectures . . . I could never seem to latch onto what was supposed to be so post-modern about it, nor could I fathom where it was I might graduate to, other than the confines of some office, and the privilege of being lulled back to sleep by fax machines and groaning copiers . . . But if not that, then it was back to the same chasm out on the streets, out in the East Village with my pals, where I wore bell-bottoms and a cowboy hat, and where I burned away those NYU stipend checks . . . What else?! I lived out real-life nightmares at gallery openings, at avant-garde art parties and poetry slams . . . I was there that night for instance, that basement in alphabet city, that white guy going nuts on his drum set with an assortment of squeeze-toys, with koosh-balls and rubber muppets raining down into the seats . . . But that was me there then, any of those nights, in that butt-ass, tight shirt, mauve stripes, like: *jazzy days, satin nights*, and while it might not have been me up on stage saying that, I was there in the crowd, and looking none-too skeptical either, as everyone around me burst into thundering applause . . .

I thought so much about art back then, that it became just like money or sex, another hump on that big burden . . . And it seemed to make no real difference after a while, which was why I eventually went to work in some of those offices . . . And why, as always, I was then belched right back onto the streets . . . I waited tables, cleaned bathrooms, cut fish . . . I toiled away night and day on warehouse floors . . . Which is how I landed here, this handful of flyers, hustling around with all these Hindus . . . *One drink, free admission*, the girl straddling the lightning bolt . . . That's us with the pink aprons on, if you can pick me out, on the corner of Fifty-Second and Eighth Avenue . . . And here's a hint: No more flared jeans . . . My technique with the flyers is to let those Indian guys do the bulk of the hustle, because they like me, and because it's hilarious to them when I dump handfuls of flyers into the trash so that I can collect my thoughts . . . Funny guys these Hindus, and how it's just a coincidence they describe their lives here as the experience of trying to escape from a dark, bottomless chasm . . . Between shifts they tell me that once they too had my same kind of delusions, but its now just *money, money, money* . . . They treat me like a spoiled prince, so I tell them one day I'll go back to that palace and for them I'll throw the doors wide, but in the meantime they can trust me when I say that chasm, that sense of depth exists not just in the downtown traffic streaming by, but because sooner or later, with or without art, Hindu or not, a man still has to find a way to free himself . . .

Tomb of Kings

More often than not you need just one friend . . . And yet my pal Valdes was like the stand-in for so many inseparable friends, and between us both it was as if we'd done every dirty job, as if we toiled then slogged for years beneath ground, only glimpsing the world above as that barely visible glow.

And *yes*, I know only Sikhs wear turbans

Like those Hindus I worked with on 8th avenue, the same as with everyone I came across in those days . . . My problem was that I was as average as the rest, and yet I underestimated that even the average man has his stupendous dreams, a fact which often jumped right up to sting me in the face.

Tomb of Kings 2:
Gold-bowelled cities

And how many nights were we down there fantasizing about lives fulfilled, watching that glow seep through the cracks? Which is what I mean when I say I pulled oars in the galleys of longships, or rather, that I slaved in the service of dreams. *That hand over hand, I once did toil in the tombs of kings.*

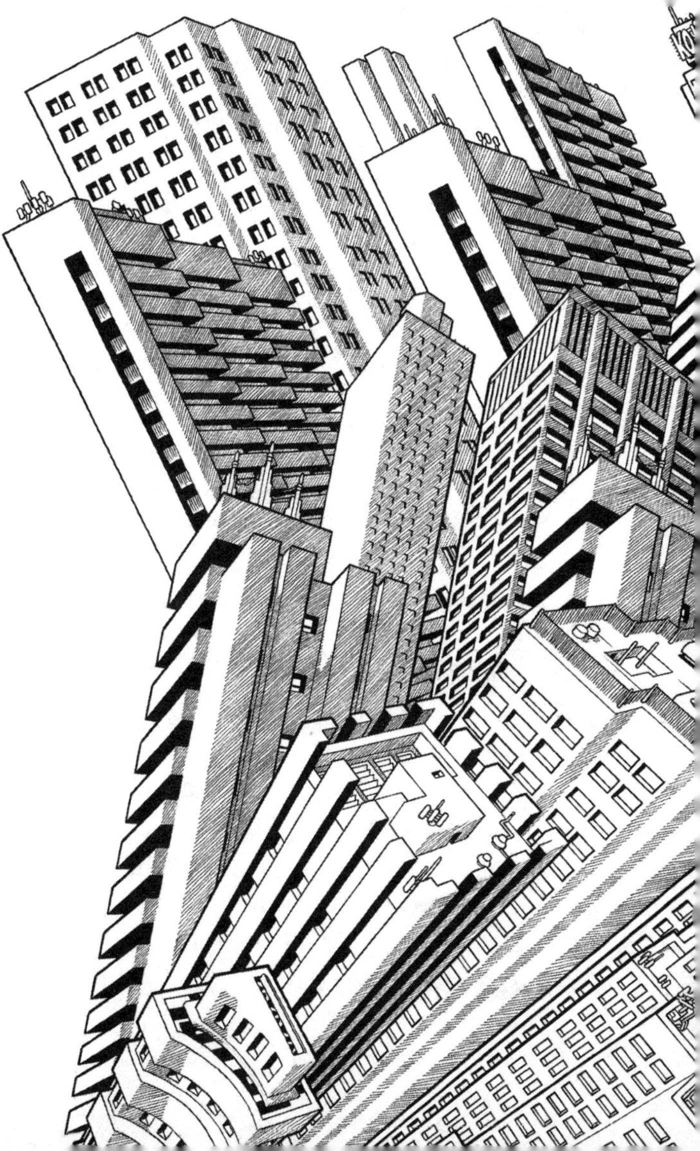

1: Call My Bluff
(New York City 2004)

Meanwhile—*Just like jumpshots, drawn lines fall and miss.* Just like those nights back in Changking, back in that box-type, tiny apartment, scratching, struggling over the drawing board, sweltering, that stink of utter defeat. In other words—*still on that 1995 tip!* Still slaving over the same silly pictures of cities exploding, of guys shooting each other in the face and futuristic prostitutes, laughing animals, huge guns and lasers, rooftop capers, of robots with plexiglass guts, flickering . . . I tried not to think about it but I had to. About how futile it was. Maybe Da Vinci never dwelled on it, but I was just a jerk with a day-job. And yet this part of it, the drawing up nights, all the ceaseless drawing, drawing, filling up every spare second—that much I felt I could do. I could die drawing. And penniless, for that matter. I could use up my last breath this way, no regrets, in that it was at least, still moving . . .

The sad fact of it though was I'd by then discovered that the real-time action of the art world took place not at the drawing board so much as behind frosted glass in ice-cold office suites. That is, you could draw all night and day but there still had to be someone you knew, some hookup into this network of art directors and editor chiefs, and maybe there wasn't much irony in the fact that few of these types could sketch out more than a stick figure. At any rate, it was no epiphany, just my suspect lack of charisma in those situations—and huge blocks of time when I think about it—flat-hued, no music, freezing in waiting rooms with my folio pressed between my knees. *Man, think!* I'd be raking myself over the coals trying to come up with some joke or tidbit, some something to help my cause. It was supposed to be all about the art, but I thought I knew better.

Or that was always my vantage point anyway, in that I rarely ever made it to the other side of that glass. I'd be sitting out there in the void, for hours, and because there was nothing else I'd begin to bite back on myself. The worst stretch was that one summer I tried to make a stand in the offices of some character named Danny Roman. Nothing dramatic, but no armchairs this time which left me sitting on the floor across from the elevators. There was the same wall of glass, and at the desk behind it was the cute secretary with the similar bob cut—*well,* similar enough, and so naturally I was thinking about the last time I saw Vanessa . . . MoCCA convention, three months back . . . I'd been in the alleyway behind the Puck building, chain smoking cigarettes, and not just because I hadn't seen her since we broke up. Not just to tide me over, for the all-day session, shuffling through the maze of tables and mountains and mountains of self-published, neon covered, existential comic books. *Yet I was the douchebag!* That's what I felt like, buffeted, trying to stay afloat in the crush of white dudes with beards and backpacks. The roar of noise in the auditorium. Somewhere in the crowd somebody was blowing a gym whistle. No matter how I positioned myself, in which direction I sidestepped and squeezed, I was still staring right into the backs of people's heads. I couldn't even see the tables, only glimpses. But I saw Vanessa; maroon tee, a picture of a ninja on it, some art-jake telling her something, and she saw me too before the crowd swallowed them up. Then minutes later, standing, by the Top Shelf table, signing comics and ringed by fans—*her fans*—which still seemed weird, I wasn't ready I guess, but there she was, apologetic smile, and opening up when she saw I didn't seem too tense about it. At least I didn't want to feel that way. You can check yourself, double back, but you can never really know if you're in fact, just pretending.

2: Call My bluff

I'd been a tool—she would say—way too pretentious, that was definitely the crux of the problem. Yet I always got that dark, greasy feeling, listening to Vanessa talk comics with her friends. Then she was always tut-tutting me, or not even, just shaking her head when I'd be on my way out to hit the streets with Valdes. But what was the difference? How was that any better or worse that their own little hang sessions, fighting with plastic swords, laughing hysterically about the plots of Japanese cartoons? Moreso than fucking, I remember the way her fingers moved over the vellum, tight, surgical lines, without pen or ink even, easy strength, even just her two fingers in pantomime, as if the picture was already there, as if all she had to do nowadays was flush it out . . . *Look, it doesn't matter how smart you think you are . . .* And this would always be while I was on the couch, half asleep, a book over my face, or watching Knight Rider, or after I'd been sitting for hours, erasing over and over the same few panels.

So you went to Hong Kong, okay, however long ago that was, and so what if it changed your life? Don't be stupid. You're not going to invent some new cosmic way of drawing comics by not breaking the pages down. You're just torturing yourself. Here, give me the pen. Blue. Look. No, look. Nobody's gonna say it but art is about rules. The rules are the format. The rules set you free. By forcing you down to a limited number of elements, and because you can't go anywhere else that's how you get better. By playing within that box. Here, from now on always start with a grid. Here. And here. Six panels, nine panels. Here. Or since you want to be a genius, try and do it without cutting off everyone's feet. Try Sixteen panels, sucker . . .

Maybe what bothered me was after a point it seemed like she was always lecturing me. The first time Vanessa drew over one of my pages with a blue pencil I remember I screamed as if she'd picked up a gun and shot me in the thigh. It was like being bullied, but then I also realized how lame that sounded. I remember that first night she gave me her number, way back when she had the wavy mane of dark-brown hair. That was before the buzz cut, then the bob; punk-rock, pink dye, before those piles of cornball minicomics she'd do, *as experiments*, before she could live without sleep and crank out three to four full pages in a day. If anything that's what I was pretending about, and there was the difference. Making it seem as if it was only her opinion against mine, just philosophy when in fact I didn't want to have to break down and admit I'd spent years lapsing and starting, wasting time, sputtering all over the page, but without that simple bit of forethought that separated real art from gibberish. Which is what my comics looked like next to hers! Like I was fooling myself, just pretending. The same with her indie-comics pals who I'd begun to despise. That gay Indian cat who was always falling all over himself giggling. Thing was, after a night of drinking beer and jumping around, him too, he could go right home on an empty stomach and draw straight through the next day as if his life depended on it. And she was right about those non-repo pencil lines too, as usual. Not that they needed to disappear—they would with the scanner— but it was just like any number of the things she tried to show me, that flew right by as I watched her work over my pages on tracing paper. Like a grade school teacher with grammar mistakes, fixing perspectives, puckered lips, her face grazing the paper. At first she was teaching me. Who knows if she felt smug about it. But then just drawing, like lightning on rails, faster than I could follow and after that certain point ignoring me completely.

3: Call My Bluff

If anything I couldn't say what was worse, trying to fit in with scenesters at the conventions, or twiddling my thumbs waiting to see art directors. I'd sit in the lobby of that office and there was almost no sound at all, just the throbbing central AC, and nothing moving after the click of the thermostat . . . Anyway, I'd decided to make a stand. Which amounted to little more than time off from my job, during which I'd arrive each morning unannounced, uninvited, portfolio in hand, at the eleventh floor office and politely ask to see a Mr. Danny Roman. Something about that office, that name in particular, if there was I couldn't tell. Much like the other offices, the dozens of calls I'd made, right down the list of job leads Vanessa had given me that day at MoCCA. The main thing I was going on was the way she'd described it to me, drawing storyboards, "urban" themed Pepsi commercials and toy designs for spinoff merchandising. Not the work itself, maybe, but that vibe, like soldiers hacking away in some great, hopeful war. I was always going to her website, not even to look at her new stuff, but to cruise the blog for talk of those times, heady days, it seemed like, racing for deadlines, drawing at breakneck speed to punk rock and afrobeat. In fact it was obviously a mistake on my part, but I couldn't help but fantasize, as if I could seamlessly insert myself into that scene, go right in, as if all that would be there waiting for me if I could only find some way to the other side of those glass doors.

Or back to that one instant, thrill on piano keys. Vanessa talking, sign-

ing books, still laughing, not quite funny, but soft-eyes—then she looks up . . . I could never seem to draw in those circumstances, in waiting rooms, so as I sat it was this one bit of tape that I chose to replay again and again. The context was that I was out of step as always! That convention had been no different really, no more dramatic than any of the choices I'd made down the line, but here again it felt awkward, shocking even, to find myself so far outside looking in.

To save the suspense, I never did get past those doors! Just two weeks sitting on the floor, regretting it, mind-numbing adventure, as if that was my full-time job. I never met that Danny Roman. Only the secretary. She'd stone-face me. I suppose that was a practiced thing, still preposterous though, as if each day she was seeing me for the first time. I'd be there in the morning, nine sharp, sipping coffee, and at some point past noon I'd go for lunch. The afternoons were worse, and after a while I had the feeling I was missing something. After all, there were no other hopefuls, not even any art-types going in and out. Because the guy was always in, that's what she said, just not quite available. A meeting. A conference call, or eating a late lunch. But no indication that I should keep waiting or not, if he would ever see me, and I'd have had no choice but to go ahead and leave if anyone had actually told me to.

And I'll admit I did take my sweet time when I went out for lunch. I wasn't usually hungry so I'd cross the street and find a bench to stretch out. And maybe that was it. The polite freeze-out. Maybe I was supposed to appreciate not having it said to my face; the mystified, cute secretary, the way they seemed to leave by some other door so they could just cut the lights on me each evening at six. I'd be on that bench, staring at the sky, and more than once I guess I did imagine going back in a blind rage. I had to go back, just like I had to keep drawing somehow, but my version of it was more like gazing down into some breezy pavilion, over the top of an insurmountable wall.

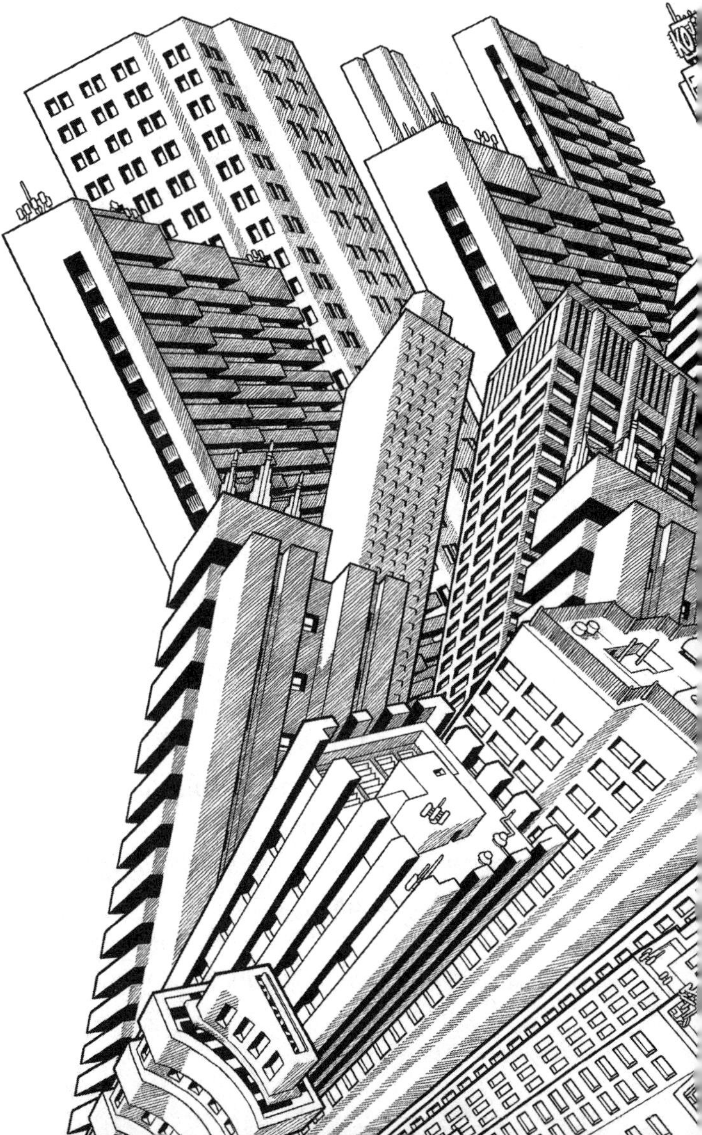

1: Colostomy

Apropos of nothing. Big grin, then pause. Then as usual it was, *yes, yes*, he knows what I mean, if for no other reason than they were always trying to get me talking about it. A loud cough rattled in my chest and I rolled around on the slats of the skid, which had them both laughing again.

"No, man." I said. *"You may have taken some rough shits, maybe, but this was a complete other thing. I must have been curled up on that bathroom floor for six, seven hours; hallucinating, crying, praying to god. I saw myself as a child, standing in the sunlight, smiling. I was afraid to do it, but after a while I got one of my girl's hand-held mirrors and actually looked down my*

own asshole, for the first time ever. Yeah, I don't know either. But, mine was all blown out and pink, monkey's ass, like some kind of weird blossom . . .

And it *was* hilarious. They'd send me and those two Salvadoran guys up to the tenth-floor warehouse on Saturdays for time-and-a-half pay. This was when I was at the bookstore on Wooster street. At first I'd been in there shelving books, but maybe I didn't fit the mold, so then I was down in the bowels, in the back rooms, sorting and busting into the cases and cases of used books that came pouring in every day. Could be that I just don't have a head for business, because it never seemed to make sense the way we'd open up the cases, resort everything and then they'd have us shuttle them right up to that tenth floor which was like a block-long wasteland of boxed books. At any rate, I suppose the real question is why El Salvador, or rather, who was doing the real work? Those guys weren't idiots either, they had the system down long before I arrived. We'd go up, spend an hour or two pushing boxes around, stacking, rebuilding the different pyramids so it looked as if we'd made a real dent, then we'd be up on that mountain of wooden skids for most of the afternoon, stretched out under the skylight. Sometimes we'd doze off. But then, those guys were also wild, impressionistic talkers, even in broken English, not only that, there were also these jags they'd go into, laughing, a little bashful about it, and they'd want to hear me keep rethreading parts of the same story again and again.

"There's a lot you take for granted, that's what I mean. Not just your ass, about the world. Or maybe that's too easy! I guess I can admit, I thought a hemorrhoid was a kind of festering sore

or something. But seeing that blossom down there, pulsing with blood, well it took me back through all those times I was sauntering around, acting cool. All those breezy moments. And back to that now, like: Wait a minute . . .

2: Colostomy

In life, but especially while working nine-to-five, there are times when the past is inescapable. For me there were phases. That summer, for whatever reason, I kept drifting back to grade school, where I was once tight pals with a guy who supposedly had a colostomy bag. The word was that he'd been born without an ass, or something, or that it was sealed up, no crack, and obviously that image alone was enough to make the guy a pariah. I say "supposedly" because it was only here, decades later that I started to peel apart some of the mythology. What I did remember was the first day starting at that school. Like with all the schools and programs and other places I'd ended up, there was that first day where gravity itself seemed to lump me in with the outcasts at the bottom of the barrel. It was an effect I never questioned, nor did I much regret it, insofar as I was still able to talk to girls. On the other hand I did feel miscast. Anyway, I'd already gotten the story about the colostomy when we met on that first day. From there we were more or less fast friends for about five or six years, and I spent most of that time half-hoping, waiting for him to snap, to crumble; anything. At the time, like with any kid that age, it wasn't cruelty, I was just unconcerned. That is, I'd never asked him directly about it, and even in my own mind I'm sure I was exaggerating the few instances of any actual bad smell. More visceral than that though, was the degree to which he was ostracized. Of course no girl would talk to him, but as time went on I also noticed the reflexive way people's expressions would begin to curdle whenever he joined a group or entered a classroom. Again, this was almost always without a whiff of anything. Even teachers would check the seats after he got up. They were discrete about it, but then that was the weight of the past, the lodestone around his neck. More than anywhere else, the irony, the truth was there in the permanent cast of his face, because it wasn't a guilty look he carried, but an irritated one, almost petulant, as if *he* was the one always recoiling from some putrid thing.

This was also the chord of my thoughts on those Saturdays beneath the skylight. It was barely a few hours of real work, but I'd be exhausted, listening to the wind through the seams of the building. I had no clue, but it was the fact I'd felt so easily superior to the guy that made me wonder where he'd ended up. And no doubt fate has some role to play with one's lot in life.

That livid feeling leads you out into the world, to break chains if you have to. With luck you can start over.

3: Colostomy

"Every comfortable surface! I'm telling you; chairs, the sofa, the dining room, the kitchen, his bedroom . . . That's right buddy, 'bolsa', I've told you about that guy I knew with the colostomy bag. I mean, his family had dogs too, but come on, that's pretty horrific. And I'm saying, everywhere, little shit-stains, shellacked into the upholstery and carpet with furniture polish. Obviously he and I never talked about it. Though I'd always be thinking: how does this guy live with himself?! How does he carry that baggage around wherever he goes?"

Doval was really the attentive one. Rapt, glassy smile. That is, to separate those two Salvadoran guys. As usual I was mainly telling it to him, *different gloss*, but the same fable, if for no better reason than his fat cheeks, the yellow in his teeth. We are who we are. And sometimes that's the only secret . . .

"But no, that's the thing and that's why I say this whole city is my colostomy bag! In fact, deep down I'm sure it's why man builds cities. Why we need them, not to discover ourselves, but as cloud cover while we're all down here, flailing around. I won't even hide that it's based on my own problems, my own POV, but I've always tried to imagine that the guy was finally able to reinvent himself somewhere, or at least get enough distance between those days where no seat was safe. Maybe he had to change his name or move overseas. Maybe he wanted to erase those days, burn the memories. I know I do. Sometimes. I can tell you, especially while we're up here, hauling boxes, sometimes I have to stop dead and cringe at

the thought of some stupid thing I did or said way back when . . . But maybe the guy made it to Brazil, where I hear they specialize in prosthetic asses. Maybe that guy is walking around now with brand-new, pristine cheeks. Two apples, with shine on them. Or maybe even here, in the city, as good a place as any to start fresh. I suppose I wouldn't recognize him if we passed in the street, any more than I'd recognize my own self years later, after countless epiphanies and whatnot. What I tell myself though, is that you have to remember, you have to hold all those terrible, filthy images of yourself firmly in mind, because each time you realize what you look like it's as if you just came up with a newer, better you right on the spot. Of course you have to do other things too—quit smoking, eat healthier, bowel control, or whatever it may be. As time wears on though, it's the power of an army behind you, and that's the guy you were back then, and before that, and before that—each next guy smarter than the rest, just a little bit, but with drum-tight assholes, waiting to be reborn . . .

Bill Bixby

I was already half-hearted about playing pranks, I knew better, but the other side of it was a day-job boredom like a caged-up, tranquilized tiger, that is, *gimmie something*. Don was another East Village refugee, a real droner, on and on, about conspiracies, the government and whatnot. He wasn't even talking to me most of the time, yet I still somehow wanted to plunge a stake in his heart. Instead of that, I brought one of those rubber bouncing balls. Right after lunch, like clockwork, he'd come in tipsy, reeking of malt beer, to blow up the bathroom in the back of the store. With the door cracked, I waited for one fart, that first rip, flicked the lights and I whipped that ball in so it would come down off the ceiling and ricochet all around the inside of the stall . . . At any rate, it was just me and Don in there, that dusty, three-room bookshop, and the owner, who sat up front behind the counter surfing porn on the internet. And no moral either, just the aftermath that was like the fog of war, avoiding eyes, no mention of it, but I was strangely consumed, even outraged, in my own mind, by the image of that guy, sitting in the dark, his punk-rock T-shirt, barbarian haircut, and gritting his teeth, straining to keep some shred of decency. By the end I'd had nightmares about it, and I spent more time than ever listening to him drone on. It seemed inconceivable there'd be no payback, so I'd go in to take my own shits and expect to be engulfed in flames or some huge explosion. Suffice to say there were other bookstores to work in. So like Bill Bixby, I moved on . . .

Timpani Drum

Like wave ripples, my pack of cracked French curves, like my stocking feet, my churning, surging thoughts, hushed on carpeted hallways. I felt the city breathe, for instance, or that could have been just me. Or like that live peacock I once saw on a leash down in Mong Kok . . . What I will say, after a while, there was no separation between the actual streets of Hong Kong and the miles of plush hallways around the YMCA. No real music either, just those things I'd seen, flickering underfoot, and it was because this was too much for me to draw at the time that I loped around all night to the imaginary tune of that timpani drum.

Buck Rogers Ring Tone

I can't even remember that girl's name. *Hope* maybe, or some kind of flower. Nor could I tell you what, if anything was all that different about it. I remember the pulse like bass heartbeats from truck windows. I was sitting in the gravel, drawing circles all over the back of a spiral notebook . . . That girl I'd already struck out with, she was from San Francisco, and Stasiu had been on her friend India all week with his usual schtick—calling, calling dozens of times, then pretending he wasn't calling and now some house-party was looming. And his schtick was a kind of Byzantine, multi-tiered labyrinth, caked with bullshit, with little bits he'd culled from the

I-Ching and books by Ezra Pound, and the way it worked, you had to wonder why the guy wasn't a closer. Valdes was a closer. Valdes fucked plenty of girls, but it never seemed to end well, nor did it ever come off smooth, and if I had to guess it was that distance that kept him an arm's length from Stasiu, in this case standing way past the fence, out on the sidewalk, hand in his pocket, staring down the line of stalled traffic on seventeenth street . . . *What else?!* India was best friends with Lindsay, and a few weeks back both of them made out a little with Mike Yeoh, same night, at some bar, which was our ticket, even though you could tell there was no chance of that happening again. For the record, you always need a ticket. If anything that was the most I knew about any of those nights, because me neither, I wasn't a closer, just a striver, because it was only ever about someone who knew someone's roommate's brother, then before you knew it we'd be back in the thick of it; couches, music, those girls dancing — same shit, but I still wasn't immune to it, none of us were, and that nth degree of separation was Goezman, who might have only been there because he was the first of us to have a cell phone, and this was 1999, that open lot between Broadway and 5th avenue, and because we weren't animals we were playing it cool, the four of us, pacing, milling around, but also like animals, like slaves, air-conditioned chimps, waiting for that *jingle-jingle* to set us free.

Empathy/remix

With drawing comics, having to struggle for it, there was an extent to which I felt I could put myself in anyone's shoes. We were all, *devalued* by life, so to speak, but in most cases I was the type to largely treat this as a blessing in disguise. Rather, there was no larger context! No wars, no children starving in other countries, nor anything aside from those boundaries separating people that seemed weirdly self-imposed. If anything I felt lucky, relieved, in the more than a few things I had in common with almost everyone I met. On the other hand, this too was the kind of overly-grand thinking that could really turn you into an asshole . . .

More Nightmares

One thing I do know is about that Japeru[1], like the rhythm of drums behind my ears, about that day-to-day spiritual warfare and waking dreams that never sleep . . . Whatever I first thought, meeting Stasiu, I can pick out clearly the image of that guy, blue velour shirt, and within ten minutes of our first handshake he gave me a poem. And make no mistake. By then I also felt I'd been going at it for years. I felt what you always feel, that what came before was nothing, that most of the guys doing it around you were

---

1 *Japeru*, and the immediately following track (*Nur Al Anwar*) that Stasiu and I always used to confuse it with, from the 2001 AUM Fidelity Release- *William Parker & Hamid Drake Volume 1: Piercing the Veil*

almost always partly faking. Flat out, I'd still admit I knew nothing about comics, much less poetry, but I guess I thought to myself that here was a guy who might bend over backwards to make you believe. Or maybe there was just no way it could sound the same on paper, and that was part of my rip on poetry, as much as it was the nerve of that guy, stuttering, drifting like a wino in front of the microphone as he read from his tattered notepads. Going on about age-old human nightmares, about sixty feet of symmetric purple, stuff like that, *dancing into it*; *Air on the edge of your lungs twirling, walking into moonshafts, into dreams the color of bone* . . . And with Stasiu it was always some weird word, mind you, like *Japeru*, some book you hadn't read, something he could see while you couldn't or some exotic-sounding concept just beyond reason. The difference between art and life was that in person you could at least tell he wanted those words to mean something, whereas on paper it was just poetry, which in my mind was no substitute for really living. That was when I had time to think about it, because, naturally I was also wading through my own delusions. I will say I wasn't all that surprised when he inevitably volunteered into the Army and was shipped off promptly to Iraq. Nor did it seem like that much of a thing when he never did come home. Years later, when I needed it most, probably, I began to hear from him again. E-mails, not letters, often just single paragraphs in which he now took great relish in describing the most mundane things, such as drinking a bottled Coca-Cola in the humid backseat of a taxicab. This was Iraq or somewhere in the Middle East, I assumed that because there was obviously no return address. At some point I stopped trying to sift through for answers. By then I'd finished grad school, I was bouncing between office jobs while still stumbling over myself at night trying to draw comics. That the real war was inside of us—on that point I felt we'd always agreed, poetry aside. But it was just like Stasiu to cloud everything up with all that nonsense then end up trying to be so literal.

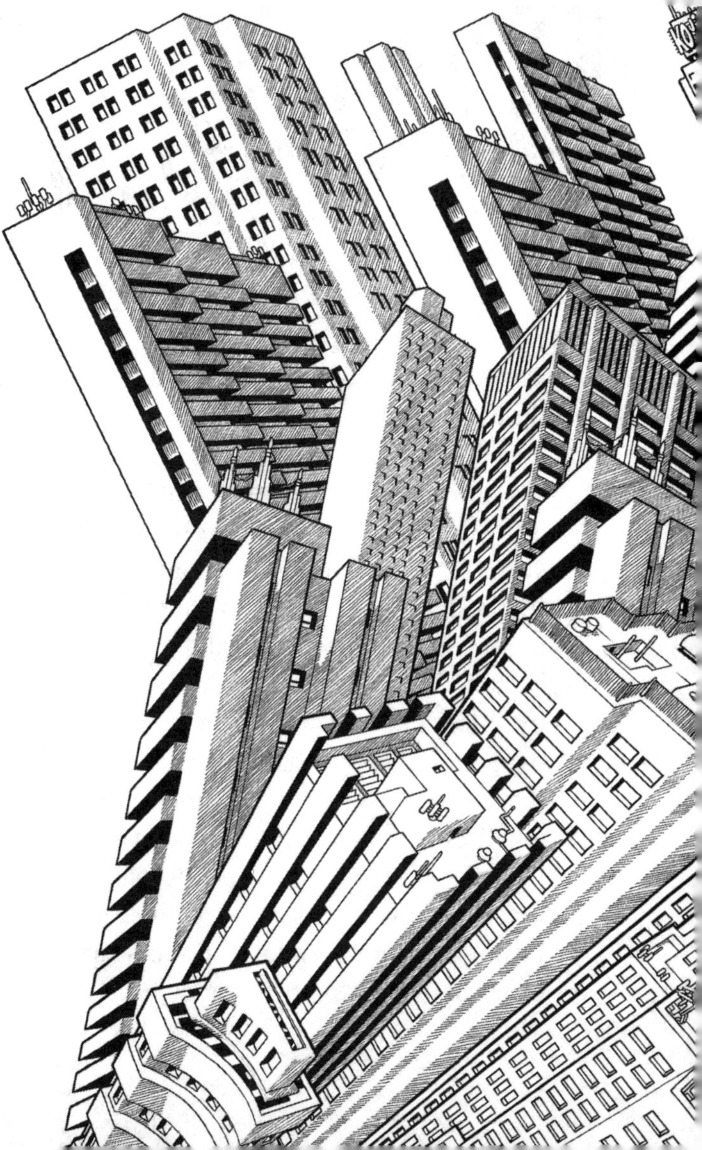

Over for Rockwell
(Hong Kong 1995)

The sad fact was the sheer amount of time I must have spent waiting, praying, paddling upstream—my faith in the concept of inspiration that almost always proved out to be fruitless. This search had become my exciting real life, while the pathetic few hours each night I forced myself to draw in turn became the farce, the myth, destroyed by experience. Clip out a clean sheet over the artboard, but it was as if I'd forgotten even how to begin. I'd also developed a hair trigger, and it took but the slightest touch of despair to blast me down that torpedo tube, out through the lobby and onto the street. Often it was the street, other times it was weaving up and down the hallways of the Temple Street YMCA, and here was the fantasy. That one could chase after inspiration. That it was only here, ten floors down from the drawing board, that I could now resume the grand purpose, feel that courage once more pumping in my veins. But also, I was in Hong Kong, alive for some good reason, and if there was in fact no real inspiration, then there had to be another way . . .

And just when you'd thought it was all over for young Rockwell— Vaulting, leaping over the fence, like counting sheep I was capable of almost anything to procrastinate, filing any act under that grand heading of inspiration. I was up, three in the morning, splashing water in my face, I was outside playing basketball in the rain. Drinking quarts, gallons of oolong tea, then jogging through the corridors in knee-high socks, Mr-arms chugging,

Black Prefontaine. I'd give myself innocuous, hopeful sounding names; *Mike Shifland, Brett Randolph,* like *Rockwell*, confusingly, but you could say that it was sometimes necessary in those days to escape my own skin just to put down the first word. Looking back on it now, this was also probably why I'd started drawing to begin with, an escape. But I was writing first, for years, stories about this and that, with little pictures and doodles of cities bridging over the margins. Or was it vice-versa? Drawing, writing, but mainly procrastinating, sitting at the desk over blank sheets then back to bed, untroubled sleep, as if I'd put away the pen for years, only to wake hours, days later in fevered sweats. I was back down in the lobby pacing, soundlessly, across the thick pile carpet with my walkman, beneath the chandelier, while the concierge and the girls behind the desk watched, back and forth, night after night, because there was definitely a part of me watching them watching me, and who knows what they thought about it . . . I was listening to avant-garde jazz, to Jamiroquai, the Stones, to Cantopop tapes I'd found half-crushed in the garbage can. Faye Wong, Andy Lau. Peter King, *Shango*, but just that opening part with the flutes. Also, Foreigner. Also some wild recording I'd found that sounded like a guy banging with his fists on a timpani drum . . . *All part of the good fight*, that's what I told myself, in fact this was just one of many chimerical quotes I jotted down while working on comics, writing right over the margins beside the panel borders. These notes then became new ideas, new credos and plans for other, never-written scripts, like riddles of science and pseudo-poetry concerning crocodiles, cyborgs, monkeys. Not only that, but other pictures, little sketches, *breakdowns*. Treatments of water, which were tricky. Futuristic skyscrapers and more mythological beasts, rearing up. Manic, half-hashed vignettes concerning flamingoes and sunken treasure. Anything at all, in fact, aside from concrete solutions to the problems that lay before me on the drawing board. Before I'd come to Hong Kong I had hardly worked a day in my life and maybe this was part of the problem. If I was a fool to believe that inspiration alone could save me then this was the ripcord process of crashing, freefall, through my own delusions. I had no worries, no real responsibilities, but the pen trembled in my hand and the world was at stake in my dreams . . .

Soothe as Excalibur

I'm gonna draw comics. For the prestige. Not for me. But for those all-over guys just like me, for every glimpse of doubt, for that stand-still paralysis and the way those moments convince you something is missing ... And something is always missing. If I can, somehow, I'll draw that on paper, and it's the one thing I might tell myself if I could go back in time. For all the people starving out there, and Yoga classes won't help. Going back to school won't help. Macrobiotic food, a finer girlfriend, more money won't help either, not necessarily. You gotta to give yourself that grand purpose, and it can be anything, in fact the more trivial the better, but you have to weld yourself to it, some big idea, to the exclusion of all else.

Because like anyone, like everyone, I guess, I still waver in and out from that feeling of being doomed to live on the outside. Man, I want to draw comics the way you'd ascend to the cloud-ringed summit of a mystical mountain. And the God's truth is you forget about getting to the top. You forget all about what you thought you wanted. You can pretend it makes you different, but deep-down, to your great relief, you begin to simply pray for another good day, one after the other . . .

Or at least this is what I'd tell myself while taking shits when I worked the Annex Bookstore on Fulton Street. It was because of those vaulted, operatic ceilings in the bathroom, and I could always hear a faint surge, like applause, from the foot-traffic on the cobblestones outside. Tiled floors and brass spigots, bathroom of champions. And I'd walk out shadowboxing, past the full-length mirrors down the corridor.

Unbelievable Worlds
(Ass is magical!)

It was her friend's birthday so of course there was a tab at some exclusive club, and she'd be there for drinks. This was at the store on Wooster street, which was Soho, and the big highlight was when they brought in this Czech girl to work the up-front counter. Or the friend that just bought a new West Village condo, she was going over to celebrate. She'd be telling the other, regular girls about her vacation, a few weeks staying with her friend in Geneva. I worked in the back, in the stockroom so I guess it made sense for her not to make eye contact. I was always turning corners right into her, and I felt bad about it, squeezing past, holding my eyes down, like: *you gotta be kidding me*—carmel skin, nine hours in the bookstore, coming from the bathroom and this bitch still smells like coconuts . . . And who were all these gratuitous friends? In spite of myself I couldn't help but wonder what that must be like. And why couldn't life just be about six-foot Euro chicks swing-walking, breezy, easing by, gliding in calf-strapped sandals down hallways and on into unbelievable worlds?

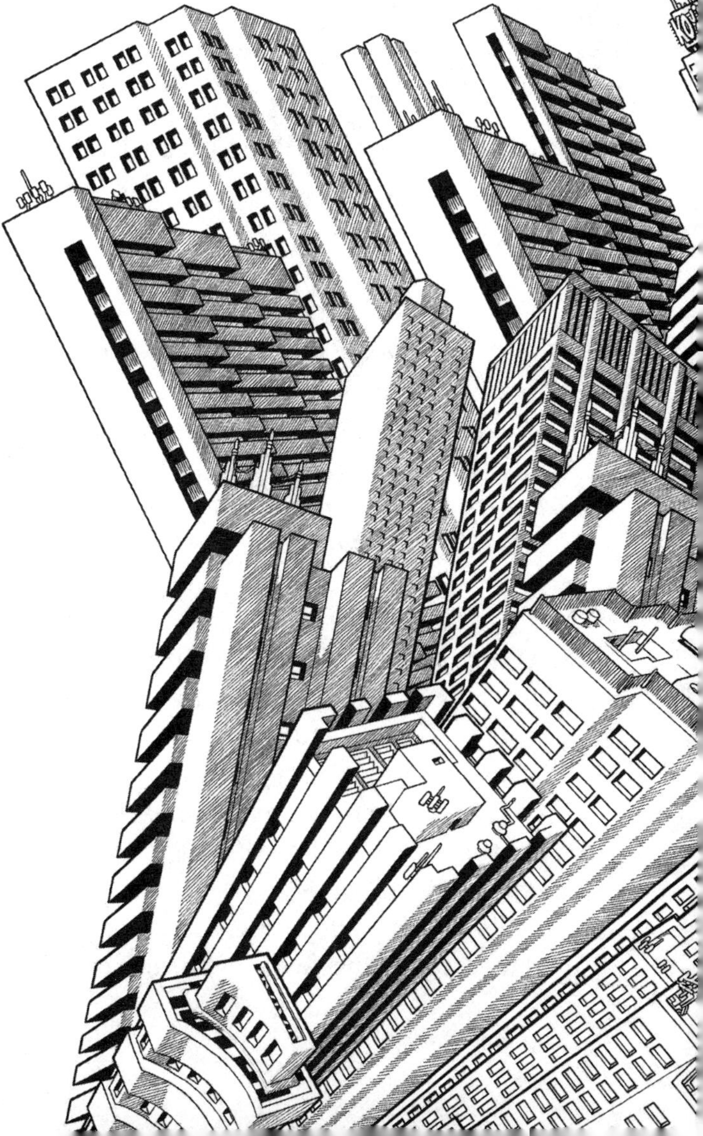

1: Streets of Rage
(New York City 2006)

So there I am, still reading the paper. Reading the newspaper like people in movies read the paper, eyes over edge, fake disinterest, looking at faces; at jaws slack, cartoon horror. I'm looking at faces, but more than that I'm counting to myself—nine, ten, twelve seconds—and what are you gonna do? At this point she's got the girl by the neck, they're slamming her against the window again, and again, the plexiglass buckling right up against my table, it's two-on-one, and I think: "Go man, go", while my feet stay glued to the floor . . .

What I remember about that summer was the fever pitch, the crazy, unbridled feeling on the streets. It was as if all of a sudden everyone had become incensed, about the war, about everything—immigration laws, bike lanes—it seemed like every next day there'd be some frantic protest march with megaphones, trumpets, and drums. And flags. Flags everywhere, every imaginable country. It was me and the Salvadoran guys, out on 17th street unloading the trucks, and every time we'd see them pass with the big El Salvadoran flag we'd run, jump out into the street and start dancing around. Then also the bumfights, which were epidemic, strangely mindless, like zombies fighting; a few minutes of some unintelligible grievance and then they'd be off, mashing each other in the face with wild haymaker blows. Or back to us dancing out there, yelling, laughing a lot maybe, but also desensitized, drenched in sweat. Doval stuffed into one of his sleeveless muscle shirts, his belly swirling around. Or weeks later when the five of us had to pull apart two of those bums, after they'd chased each other in circles for what seemed like twenty minutes, while we stood watching, hypnotized.

Go man go! Right from reading the paper, to the back of this woman, like holding onto a bucking rhino. That's out, through the door of the restaurant, and before I've any idea of what I plan to do, I leap onto her back as she bangs the girl once more into the glass. Struggling, staggering on the sidewalk in a heap, and that's what I get for feeling guilty, like a spectator in life. Hot breath in my face, screaming, this sweat-slick Spanish woman with a boxer's neck. The girl is also screaming. The woman has her by the hair in a deathgrip. I'm also holding her hair, between her bleeding scalp and this woman's fist, and the shocking thing is we're all looking each other in the eyes, with blood over everything, our hands and wrists, on the girl's forehead and down, staining deep into her yellow camisole shirt . . .

Or weeks after that bumfight, I was in the doctors office and again, just watching, sitting there as an old cripple stumbled over his walker and crashed to the floor at my feet. That summer, in the middle of a shouting match about something, I remember Jackie caught me with a hard slap on the jaw that dropped me to one knee. The Wednesday after that, in the bookstore, a guy from the web department snapped over some trifle, got up and stormed out, pulling down a huge stack of mail orders in bins—*crash!* The war in Iraq, the housing crisis, gas prices were soaring. I'd been back working at Rowell's for less than six months and that was also the summer the building's foreman dropped dead on the sidewalk from a coronary. Rather, he dropped to the pavement foaming at the mouth, choking on his own tongue from what I heard, and I could imagine what he felt, not unlike a kind of blinding rage, the same as that old man in the doctor's office, his face flushed dark red, angrily flailing and gasping on the floor—but furious, slo-mo and swollen up, like the last few seconds of something catching up to you, like death and destruction, and the prelude to that was the buzzing all around us as we worked up on the third floor with the windows open, listening to the crowds of people stomping and roaring in the street.

2: Streets of Rage

No, officer, I don't have an attitude. No. No, I don't. I'm not trying to pretend I wasn't out there. No idea what it was about. I don't know that girl. Don't know any of them. Like I said. They had her against the window. Okay, no. Right there. Her. She had her by the hair. Then some kid with cornrows came up and kicked her on the ground. That's what I mean about two-on-one. What was I supposed to do? As soon as I came out the kid took off running. I don't know. Not from me. Look, no way was I gonna fight her. I was just holding onto the-

Here again, the cop shushing me. Hand in my face while he chatters into the radio. I'm back in the restaurant, at my table, cold chicken wings and fries on the plate in front of me flashing blue and red. Outside the cop cruisers parked in a swarm all over and on the sidewalk. They've got everyone against the cars, lined up. Talking to the girl who is sitting on the pavement, still bleeding, angry, crying. The same few questions over and over again.

I told you I don't know that girl. Alright. From the beginning. I was sitting right here, eating. Then over there, him, red shirt, he comes in with her. I assume that's his girl. They're also eating. Okay, that's when that big bitch comes up. She's with the old man, and they see these two through the window. She and the girl know each other and right away they're going at each other in Spanish. Big shouting match. At first the old man is keeping them apart. Then the girl says something he doesn't like and he shoves her, hard, back into the restaurant. The boyfriend jumps up, goes for the old man. Three of them are fighting, wrestling in the doorway, then those Chinese cooks run out from the back and push the whole pileup through the door, into the street. Then after that who knows? All those neighborhood guys were coming up off the street and jumping in. The kid throws the old man on a car, then he's fighting another guy, everyone's screaming in Spanish and running around nuts. As soon as the girl runs out, that bitch grabs her by the hair and starts giving it to her up against the window. Like I said, who knows, she might've deserved it. I sat there for as long as I could stand it, then I went out and jumped in, and a few minutes after that was when you guys showed up . . .

I try to finish eating, no taste, cold bites, sitting for hours afterward in that Chinese restaurant, my arms and fingers still tingling, my t-shirt torn and stretched out like a tarp. The Chinese cooks still piled up in the window, watching the police, the scene outside, then back to me, staring, then the weird silence gets to be too much, so I roll up my newspaper and it's back, onto the street, between two of the cop cruisers, and there goes that woman, in the back, in cuffs, huge neck, eyes affixed to nothing, ice-cold and waiting. Then on the subway, trundling home, just looking at the scuffed toes of my shoes. Then at home, sunk into the couch with the windows open, the fan going, and I don't want to talk about it, I don't want to wake Jackie or Zhanna, but then there she is, Zhanna, rubbing her eyes with little fists, crawling onto my lap, sighing, sleeping again, and since I'm just an average loser with a shitty job at a bookstore, I'm struggling, I'm also thinking ahead though, because she can't say full sentences yet, and for her the days are still exciting and packed, and they don't drain the life out of her, and since it's something I often wish someone had tried to do for me, I figure there must be some way, some words to explain it, *and Zhanna, baby, whatever you think*, you've got to keep all the everyday, ordinary disaster from crippling you.

Strange Hush

I got used to all the bums, the shuffling, wild busking on the subways, the circus-style panhandling—but mostly just the ceaseless, driving samba of loose change in cups . . . There was so much about the pace of life in this that it felt cold, even ominous, on occasions, when I would come up onto silent, empty streets.

Go-Backology

Buttress my days and nights against the fact you waste years of life in transit. From one thing to the next. From one way of thinking, to the TV shows you like, to doubts about your girlfriend, your job, then also these pointless revelations on art. Which if you think about it, that's just another kind of prickly religion demanding absolute faith. *And Sakura, I'll even give up on the idea of becoming some great genius . . .* All that back and forth, then out of bed as if tossed from a turbulent sea, when what I really like is that resolute feeling of drawing comics, pen to paper, like landing on some hasty idea then refusing to budge.

Art is Life: *Compression*

Come to think of it, you must have started drawing before anything. You mean, before you wrote your first word. Because drawing is elemental, instinct, but also in that obvious way you still have to learn how to do it . . . Having watched your own daughter draw, to you, it now makes more sense, watching her, like first steps, the first of many things, maybe, that nobody tells you, you could do without it, *just fine*, only the idea nags at you. From standing to walking, to running—*big jump*, then drawing comics, but somewhere in between as well, you had to have picked up that ballpoint pen, and you must have wrapped your fingers around it. *New world?* If it did seem that way there was no magic in it. Because you were at the same time also learning colors, numbers, shapes, how to climb stuff, then eventually how to write letters, then cursive, then how to hate—homework and people, because that's in all of us, not hate but stupidity, *pull back*—but also to fake confidence, even when you were wrong, to kick that soccer ball, climb the jungle gym, to chase girls around the playground, that is, until the whistle, then turn around and run like crazy while they chased after you.

All this seemed futile, a little robotic, back then, that much you remember. First a steep fall—the learning curve, they call it—first you feel like a fool doing whatever it is, that's the futile part, then the repetition, that endless chopping, chopping, and one way or another you have to submit to it. *Chopping it up—That's how you remember Mrs. Hanson's first grade* *class, with all that fucking seatwork . . . * Writing in cursive, for instance, made no sense to you, like blurred sandscrit, same as with algebra, with physics lectures years later, none of which you really learned, which never mattered, just the way everyone else seemed to be humming along, so you tried to race your pen across the paper with the same chopping strokes . . . *It's in that sense you want to credit intuition for everything. The looping shapes of those algebra notes that seemed more like pictures, emotions. That glimpse of yourself, fully-formed, bursting with ideas. What you rarely think about is how many directions you were forced in, the skill-sets you picked up under duress. But all that counts, maybe even more than what you felt inspired to do. In effect that is your underworld, your invisible city. Those degrees of reluctance. Not just the time or two you had your heart broken, but also the fact that* *you cried, for years, whenever you had to eat broccoli. Not only that but you hated art classes, couldn't stand em', if you can remember. What else have you forgotten? Comics you say, as if that explains everything. Meanwhile what are you doing with life? Who are you doing it for, and why?*

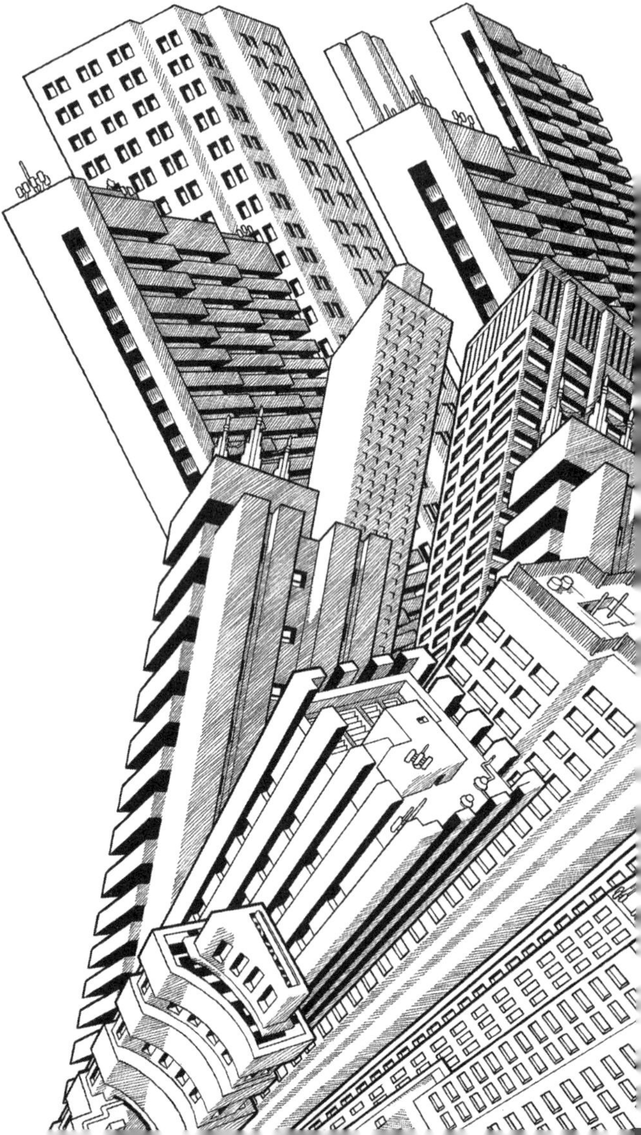

1: China Dog Syndrome
(Hong Kong 1995)

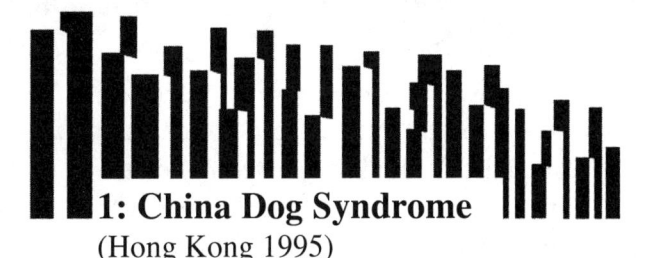

I was lost in thought that first time, perched on a cement k-rail and one of them caught me, just it's face, Labrador mutt, it's wet nose against the chain link between full-length wooden shutters, and one loud bark that threw me over backwards . . . That was somewhere in Sham Shui Po. I'd come out from the maze of tenements and construction sites; high-rise, half-built shopping centers and who knows, condos I guess. Out under the streetlights along the footbridge, the pale green railings. Down the steps, vault the trash bin, the lot across from Lai Chi Kok fairgrounds, and by then I'd always be running.

Berwick Street, cross beneath the on-ramp. Path of offset concrete slabs, the back alley between two tenement blocks, so all I could hear was the groan of AC fans. *And sometimes it was as if I was walking to keep my thoughts in place, at bay, like treading water. Even in the dead of night, certain blocks were packed, bustling, but around the next turn, silent streets, just me and those dogs loping behind fences . . .*

One conceit about art is that you gotta live it. In other words it wasn't enough to sit in my room and draw comics, I had to get out there and move, double-clutch, dive right into that nameless skelter of Chinese sidestreets. The catch was that you were looking for something new, to see the unseen, and this was the rhythm of my feet while each next thing bled into the rest. At first I'd been taking notes. Or trying to, one of those fifty cent memo pads. After a while though, all those pointless notes and sketches piling up became yet another set of rules to shake off and leave behind, old news, or worse yet another level, another city, a riddle, there like a brick in my sweaty pockets. What I couldn't escape, I suppose, was the idea that I was at all times moving against the great tableau of things already done and seen before, and if anything this was the part which made the game difficult.

Or back to Berwick, Pak Tin Street. Walking beneath the crisscrossing, merging, smooth-brushed eaves of the highway overpass, with ink-blue night coursing through the seams. From there I could already see the glow of Lai Chi Kok, like a huge furnace buried behind the tight-packed blocks of Sham Shui Po.

Before that I'd follow the MTR route. Prince Edward to Ki Lung

Street, my bridge through Mong Kok. And that was miles and miles of shuttered shops, doorways with draped-over tarps, wet concrete and lit-up alleyways in between. Into Mong Kok from Nathan road, the street you see on the postcards. That sense of the infinite, bouncing on the balls of my feet. Left on Nathan from Temple Street, the Hong Kong Y, glass front, eight stories down from my room. And each night I'd burst through those doors, patting my pockets—*Cigarette?* Resume.

2: China Dog Syndrome

Or, Berwick street, back in as if from a dream. I'd crouch by the hole in that fence with my hand out, whistling, because I couldn't fathom it, and it seemed like the easiest, most natural thing in the world for them to step through, run free . . .

Not just the black lab, but dozens of them, every time I tried a shortcut; drowsy, bullnecked, off-colored mutts, half the time covered head-to-toe in sawdust—not to mention the little combai that tried to take a bite from my ankle. And I'll admit, one of my first real disappointments about Hong Kong was discovering that these dogs I'd been seeing had all been trained or put there by the construction companies operating on each site. Which was much less mythical, less *Chinese*-sounding, of course, than my own far-fetched ideas. Add the fact of how bowled over I was by everything. So mystified! By so much going on, the thought of it, *huge city*, with so many schemes and frantic people, Chinese and otherwise, laughing and lounging and rushing around. To put a tag on it, I was the worst kind of artistic douchebag for those first few months in Hong Kong, and it seemed plausible then for there to be these nomadic troupes of stray dogs throughout the city, migrating from site to site. But beyond that I was being drawn out, lured by the feeling there was something in the streets I needed to bottle up, take with me, that I could hoard to myself. So I'd be out there with the notepad, but mainly just moving, thinking, roaming like one of those dogs, touring around inside half-built, sprawling ideas with no real way yet to make sense of them.

Then again, you have to catch yourself. There was one shortcut, one site I remember; striped tarpaulins all around the block, draped behind huge splits in the fencing. Three dogs in there, who never barked, or not much, but they chased me around like devils, and it was errie how they'd always pull up short just as I'd run through one of the holes in the fence. It would be too much, probably, too far to say that in drawing comics I felt like some brainwashed Chinese dog, but this was a thought I returned to over the years as I tried to discipline myself. The irony is that you always expect art to feel different, and maybe it should, but to me that discipline was like coming to a dead stop in front of an invisible wall. This was years later when my whole life was chained to a desk, struggling with rulers and perspective, when I had no excuse anymore not to learn the actual math of depicting cities. After that there were only spurts of freedom, little delusions, and it was here I'd imagine that phalanx of dogs gliding around me like shadows in loose formation, hurdling tools and buckets, jogging through the struts.

The Guillotine

First of all, the difference in how we were dressed. This guy shows up to meet me like it's the first day of gradeschool; a real tight T-shirt on, with some sort of cartoon robot, with Airwalks and huge headphones connected to his discman. Not that I wasn't also dressed like a jerk, but it was another genre completely, and that was something I never thought about back in Iowa City . . . Dustin, or "Rush Hour", that was his name around the dorms. Fact was, I never took him seriously until it came out that he was from Hong Kong, which in those days was like telling me about fabled cities of gold. But then, standing there on the quad overlooking the Star Ferry, he was probably the one Chinese guy least likely, in that entire city, the least well-equipped to foray into the kind of adventures I'd thrilled on about in school. Thinking of Hong Kong, I'd pictured Rush Hour out on some mythical dancefloor, grinding in an undulating crush of Miss Asia contestants. I suppose this was in deference to his ambient synth music, his Japanese New Wave cinema, that and the drum program he was working on that had something to do with Ayn Rand. Even the part in his hair seemed to fall flat in a way that was lusterless, eerily content, bowl-cut over wire-rimmed specs. Not gay, not repressed, but way too detached. In fact this was almost the first time I'd taken a real look at him, having been friends for years, thousands of miles from where we met. It wasn't fair, but I still felt kind of deflated, trudging ahead of him down the tarmac while he rummaged around in his backpack with the ten thousand straps.

Hong Kong

It sounds good in books. And we like to pseudo-analyze, I guess, overthink it, and assume the keys to everything lie in the past. But for what I've found, I'll say, from combing those depths, you might as well go in for vague truths and flashbacks obscured by fog. You might as well go to a psychic, or a witch doctor . . . Likewise, from the couch, I can tell you my earliest memory, at eight, maybe nine years old, being led through the streets of Hong Kong by my father, and I think he believed I'd turn out better, smarter somehow, if I was able from an early age to see the world. So I was an optimist, plucked from the suburbs, but I'd have been lying if I said I could pick out some great insight impacted on me from so much traveling. I remember being adrift, a coconut, floating for miles, over those childhood years like eons, and if anything it was this same buoyant, super-light feeling, of moving without moving, that right or wrong, I came to attach to the experience of living in cities. Hong Kong was one of many stops along this tour. New cultures, strange food, that's me with my mouth full, talking, eating and chopping it up with people in places like New Delhi, Bangladesh, in Benin, and the sense of alienation wasn't all that different from being back home in the suburbs. Yeah, I knew the difference, but I could also admit the feeling was essentially the same. On a short leash from the hotel, out there with snacks, or coins jingling in my pocket. A rolled-up comic book. With my father seeming to tower over everyone in the entire country. From that early perspective, the city itself, at least in my mind, was no more complex than a bare patch of asphalt on which to stretch out and observe the passage of clouds.

Yet here I was, on the same beat, twelve years later. Stone lion with the weird, Asian mustache. I must have passed that thing thirty times in the course of a week. I could say only that Hong Kong had become like a mantra, a gnawing, reverberating thing. An instinct. Loose spiral, cement steps, off from Austin road, curling into the maze of glittering, veering sidestreets that nicely summed-up the shift down from dream, from those Iowa City nights turning on the bunk in my dorm room thinking about, what, Chinese girls? It was more than comic books, or about some movie I'd seen. Like piled metaphors, a mashup, like impacted teeth, rather, buildings, pillars of city, shifting, never still, corridors opening, sliding, for whatever reason—this was now the legend, and my guide for solving problems, moving through life. Though I doubt it was what he meant, way back when, my dad, how he'd explain things. That it was some people more than others, maybe. But some of us were meant for cities . . .

Hide if You Have To

Or for instance—*what did guys like him think about?* That's what I asked myself, while we sat like goons in the Front Street McDonalds, or in his room at his parent's house. It was what I'd always wondered about Rush Hour, what I could never figure, no matter which way I tried to take it. His parents were religious, Chinese Christians, which seemed a little spacey, and maybe that played a part. His father was an English professor at the international school. My own father was a man who worked like a machine from dawn to dusk and came home every night to sit alone in front of the television, a man who had pulled so far back from the thought of adventure that it might have been enough to explain why I was then so consumed by life on the street. Meanwhile, who knows what Rush Hour thought about? Not that he wasn't unnervingly full of talk at times, plenty of bland conversation, and in that same monotone, about this or that, about some movie or some something that neither of us really gave a fuck about. I'll admit I often felt like shaking him, slapping him across the face. Or maybe not that far. At any rate, he never seemed to get tired of baby-sitting, following me around, and we must have covered miles of empty corridors, in and out and beneath the streets of Kowloon. Dingy, blue-tiled hallways, of closed doors hung with clean briefs and undershirts out to dry. What else?! That girl we saw, barefoot, gone around a corner, in a shuffle of other, heavier feet, wearing a sequined dress underneath a raincoat. *See that?* Or down on Tung Choi, the all-night markets, where, after a little back and forth between Rush Hour and one of the vendors, the man ran around turning the little cranks on the backs of all the toys until the table was ablaze with jumping robots spitting sparks . . . What I mean is that these were instances where I'd have been laughing hysterically, or shouting, probably, or romping around, were it not for Rush Hour, Dustin, tight smile with no teeth, *and if that doesn't light you up inside*, I'd think, then what else was there, and we were a couple of spooked birds, glancing at each other, hands in our pockets, still waiting for something to happen.

Hong Kong/1995

I liked the idea of a city atop hundreds, thousands of canals of streaming light. A city, in fact a multitude of cities, bisected, stacked, jammed together, going in all directions at once and with every kind of hustle thriving in between. The problem was how badly I wanted it to be different, revelatory . . . No doubt it became as much about the world around me as it was that world I was hoping for, those dreams I thought about, struggling, doing pull-ups, on the fly, from scaffoldings over the sidewalks. I'd roam around all night, notepad in hand, and even then it was as if I was searching for something more profound to say about it.

Technological Laser

Open again onto Terra Firma, my world outside of life— impregnable, night-lit avenues, onto looped, winding streets, blurring to the next, the spaceship glow from the dash, breeze pleading from the slit in the window, the shrieking engine, the beaded figurine swinging from the rear-view . . . I'm not drunk, but dog-tired as I slosh against the back seats of the cab. Not a fool, just used to, and by now even comforted by the relentless way the drivers want to get you with the same roundabout hustle, this psychotic, high-speed touring all over the map. Next to me against the headrest is about everything I own, zipped-up in a duffel strained to the seams, and tied to that is the sense that none of this is real enough, not yet, not the teahouse, sitting with my notepad, like some anthropologist, certainly not the Temple Street Y with its maid service and turned over bedspreads, though that I could fix at least, *cue the rush, heist flick*, stuff my bag then check out, then a cab back into the flotsam sea of streaming lights, hurtling across lanes, downshifting, and what I do know is I've got to go deeper.

Shazambro!
(New York City 2004)

Ah, man. This guy, look at him. And you gotta give it up. Just yesterday I was on the main floor doing a little survey, and if the rumors read, then this motherfucker's touched on almost every girl around here worth getting for the last five years! That girl in the art department, you remember, looked like, uh, Winona Ryder. Or how about what's her name, that six-foot Dominican piece. And look at this guy. Balding, right up the middle. Look at that gut! He's been wearing that inside-out lightning bolt t-shirt four days at least, and I should know, I've been doing double shifts. You remember that brunette with the ringlets they sent up to the web department? Yeah, with the rack, she'd be wearing that tight, flower-print cocktail dress, man, kaboom! Well, word is, naturally, Zambro had her all open down there in the stacks. All over those tits and everything. The whole business got too close for comfort, he cut her loose, so then she went nuts. Crying, whatnot, yo, it was a mess. Which was why she got transferred upstairs all of a sudden. Wait, here he goes . . .

He passed, and it was the same each day, every week, giving us the head-bob, walking with that little bounce, beneath the awning, down the row of book carts, patting his pockets, and Valdes rushed to take out his own cigarette.

I'm gonna light up right when he does, wait . . . But seriously, could you even imagine a girl like that getting all heartswept over you? Those lips? The heat of the moment? Think about that. How tall is that guy, like six-one? I told you he's been wearing that same shirt all week! Oh yeah man. Some guys know how to live.

Tomb of Kings
(part 3)

Here's another one, bling-bang clip, that excitement, off the subway, sea of bodies, seething flesh, up from the eighth avenue platform and adrift. That's me and Valdes, jogging those stairs, rushing out to where I don't remember, but there was that tagged-up, big banner cell phone ad with the famous actress, that whatshername, her hips, her huge-huge grin over the shoulder, selling the dream, not just shilling but digging deep, her face against the phone, sighing, she's telling you, her fat ass there, body waving hello, and it wasn't just us, that part of the poster already punched through from the hundreds, thousands of dudes maybe, every week, around that corner giving her the Friday night high-five . . .

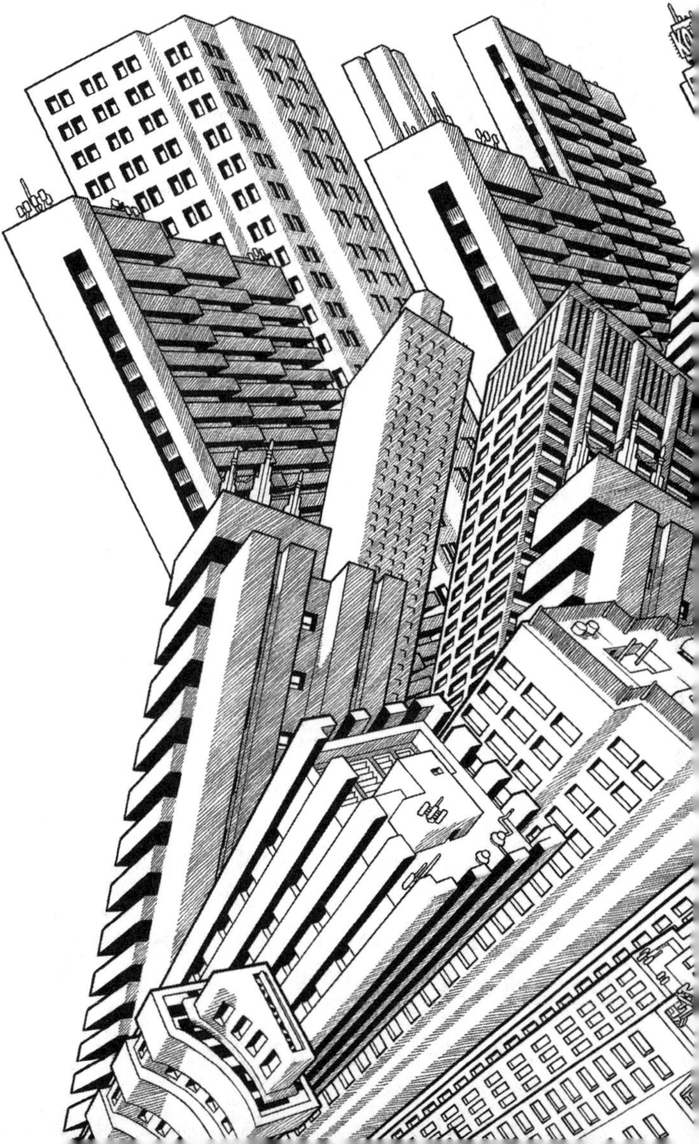

1: The Vegetal Kingdom
(New York City 2006)

I get blank stares when I bring it up. Like, *who cares*, right? But you wont ever convince me there's anything worse about being a bum than the sheer loneliness sometimes . . . I once saw a white bum on the platform at Union Square, 11pm on a Saturday night—he must have had elephantitis or something—with hordes, throngs of well-heeled party goers waiting for the train, while this guy is lurching around like a zombie, pants down, screaming and moaning, cupping his one huge, watermelon-sized testicle, and the restrained panic as everyone tries to pretend nothing's nothing, shuffling to get out of his way . . . Or especially during the summer, when I'm delirious on no sleep, roaming around with just lint in my billfold. Or when I've been really busting my hump on the job. That's when I start to resent these guys, shuffling and whining, making a show of it, crying poverty, then the next minute back to whistling about town, fancy-free. I can remember it dawning on me too. I realized the ones I see are usually the same bums I've always seen, and in the same spots, their turf, eating Thai food handouts from the college kids, which are better than the food I usually eat. Which isn't so bad, I suppose, not like the ones who set up the little table with the 10 gallon-jug full of coins. That is to say, *motherfucker*, why don't *you* work all day and I'll perch the sidewalk looking at girls, and when you pass you can just add *your* paycheck to my huge cauldron full of cash. Or in the mornings while I'm trying to read comics on the subway, the trio of Mexicans wearing green sashes, strumming guitars and singing at the top of their lungs. *You want some change? Get that accordion out of my face!* Or the one tipping his hat, holding the door as I walk out from the ATM. Or the guy pretending to be a cripple, first with crutches then with a wheelchair, using his tip-toes to help maneuver alongside cars waiting for red lights. That look on his face, part Ghandi, a touch of Jesus on the cross. *Man, somebody round up these guys and put em' to work in a factory . . .*

At some point though, it occurred to me that the streets are actually teeming with bums. It may seem like a jump, but what I think about is the fact that no one in their right mind, not one of those slaves was the least bit interested in building any of those great Egyptian pyramids. That is, great to reflect on, in museums, in books, but how about the weight of a two-ton brick of limestone across your back? And in those days, who else was it, humping those blocks up ramps, who else, but the vast army of resigned wage slaves, that is, you and me; up at the crack of dawn, trundling, en masse on the train, then choking down billions upon billions of bagels, gallons of coffee, that is, *try and disguise the whip*, choke it down, *but snap to it*, so those wheels of civilization wont miss a beat, so they keep right on turning . . . I think about the way civilizations are always built, and now maybe it's not so far-fetched to opt out and start begging for change. And yet still, it's another big jump from that to the kind of insidious routine of these same, East Village bums. Either it's some song and dance act, or the boho sidewalk routine, trying to hook me into talking with some bit of vague philosophy. *And who do I look like?!* After ten years of listening to the same few chatty bums strike up and introduce themselves again and again, I suppose by now I look the same way they do to me, not so much as people, more like the city itself, like low clouds between the buildings, like the steam coming off the streets. That is, *get mad about it if you want to.*

2: Vegetal Kingdom

And who else?! What I wonder about is now vs. the past, if in fact the time-clock, our high-definition TVs, the itemized deductions on our paystub— if any of that really makes it easier to swallow . . . I wonder about those days for instance, in cities with names like *Iztapalapa*; dark, Aztec days, down stone alleyways, in the shadow of temples, where average guys like me might find themselves dragging around canoes filled with human excrement— *And like that, every job I'd had always seemed so dismal, but what was the alternative?* That's what I thought to myself—and it was almost funny— listening to the escalating pitch, the building rage in the voices of bums as I flatly refused to hand-out money. But then also I figured the least I could do was let them air it out, maybe because in life we all exceed our grasp to an extent, and so that's what I called myself doing, *humanizing*, often just standing there in Union Square, or out on sixth avenue, hands in my pockets, with some tattered fool trying to reason with me, shouting and spitting in my face . . .

Who else but the guy, swaddled in long toilet-paper rags, filthy mummy, or the fat drunk, his beard and red hat, and almost doubled over, leaning forward as he stumbles past me each morning down Wooster street . . . Then on the other side of all that is Black Santa. On the upside of all these squatters and mendicants and would-be former rebels. Like most of the East Village bums, he trawls the loose circuit between the few remaining old bookstores that still buy the stuff he culls from dumpsters. Black Santa, skeletal guy, lame leg, side-saddle on his bike, his route that runs right along 4th avenue, by the freight entrance where we wait for delivery trucks. And like with a number of my busom pals, it's nothing specific. He'll glide up off the street and because there appears to be nothing ill at ease about him, you also, palpably, feel more relaxed. The guy's no comedian, but you laugh around him, and I often find myself outside the freight, loitering with Black Santa, saying nothing, but with a smirk on both our faces, as if there's just something about watching the traffic go by. I can't even recall exactly why the name, *Black Santa*. The leitmotif, I suppose, is that it's not too far-fetched for me to see some of myself in everyone, especially those whose one sin from the start was thinking they'd become great artists. You can see it in the way all these New York village bums can do something; some can sketch, on tattered cardboard or on the sidewalk with colored pieces of chalk. Others carry trumpets or guitars, and failing that, most can dazzle you with some flare of ingenuity. Black Santa is a painter. Or maybe that's what he thought he'd be, way back whenever it was he first came to New York. Now he's another one of those toothless guys, and I'll admit it's definitely because it very well could be me that I give him the thumbs up as he hobbles in off the street. He was beaten up recently, and there's still dried blood caked on the bald crown in his nest of dreadlocks. His shirt is loose, ripped, his pants are stained, and I think what I like about him is that he seems somehow culpable, he expects no sympathy for his condition. He's never asked me for money either, which helps. Instead he scoops out and begins to rifle the contents of his pockets. Like me, *just lint*, along with a few pennies, a faded lottery ticket and what looks like a crack pipe. He sighs at these, and because he's still smiling, I also burst out laughing . . . Then again, it's not just Black Santa. I suppose I still do give money to bums, and it's because they might be the only ones of us truly living free. And that's what my dollar is for. Maybe I want to know if that freedom still feels worth it.

Get to the Chopper!

It was my own fault. In that I felt the need to spring to the phone no matter the hour, no matter what, that gnawing, seething sense of isolation, to the extent I almost felt guilty having been sound asleep at 2am . . .

"Man, Blue, you awake? So yeah, I was watching Predator, on cable. Haven't seen that since, I don't know, ten years. And maybe it's an easy call, but you ever get the feeling with that stuff, like you're watching some stag film on the DL? Remember that scene where the Indian guy, out of nowhere he cuts off this fat vine and starts sucking that white syrup squirting out of it? What the fuck was that? Or those scenes where Arnold's like, just gazing at his

men jumping around instead of looking for the Predator?"

"Wait. Cable—what? " I sat up on the futon, blinking.

"Think it's a reach? I'm telling you, Some of that shit was uncomfortable to watch. That part where they're all standing there pumping their rifles, shooting off into the jungle? The camera pans over their straining faces? That's gay! C'mon man. You can say it . . .

Butyrate Fuse

The lanceolate rush of ruled lines, of sunsets, of inked suns setting in pencil, of minutes, hours and days, right to this point. The something of something, get it? The butyrate fuse. The eclectic substrate of this and that, of childhood, your little tragedies, and you've got nothing but mean-time consider it. The tension, as always is also music, a kind of bad poetry, while the drawing itself is still pure science, like numbers, hard to crunch . . .

And Sakura, if nothing else, I'll take comics by titration drip, drip by drip, or that clack, clack of the wall-clock hands, in my ears and climbing like the roar of a hurricane. Sakura, what's left but those comics I said I'd draw, those legends, and how legendary does it seem to imagine me here sitting in my long-john underwear, still drawing, but you'd know better than I do if I'll ever make good on that promise. Not just the clock but the sound of my neighbors downstairs fucking, the tump, tump of the headboard, reminding me just how little things change. That headboard, the bare white walls doming in on me, the cold wind racing up against the bricks outside. What remains Sakura, is the same game of patience. Start with blue pencil, rule out the page, then, new sheet, break down the panels in ballpoint pen. Meanwhile, wars are being fought, empires are crumbling, people are out there falling in love and dying, dust to dust. Now back to the ruled board, rough out the figures. New sheet, work out the faces, the positions of fingers, details on draperies and guns, plan out the lighting—in fact expand this step to encompass life and death because of how long it takes, because of the agony in the countless sheets I draw all over then crumple up and toss to the floor. In fact Sakura, this is the only step, and my only night alive, night after night, and if you do ever think about me, this struggle is what I'd like you to remember . . .

The struggle. Perastalsis—no, slower, the formation of canyons, drip by drip. A single page drawn in a month, or three, and that's with barely enough time to breathe. That's underwater time. That shipwreck noumenality check-back, pause. Abstemious, hungry ghosts. Cerbic fishes. Vincible doubt . . .

The Rub

Sakura. Rarely in life do we know the *"whys"* of what we do. There's the rub. You can't afford to think too much, so you stagger on, for years, while your other options all dry up. After a while, you really don't have a choice. What else can I say about it? I'll finish a page and I sometimes dream of being struck down and killed. Wake up. Go to my job, come home, sit down, and because I'm still alive, I keep trying to draw comics, night after night.

Cats That Walk Through Walls

At any rate, I'll be the one to tell you, I'm no Jim Lee. But in eighth grade that was the man, the number one artist I'd ever heard of, and that included Michelangelo and Rodin. Even now, the action comics you see still look like Jim Lee drew them, but to get the real idea you gotta go back, you gotta look at those Uncanny X-men, those Punishers from the late 80's—even if you don't like comics, or you hate superheroes, that's the thing now I know—you can still go back to look at the movement, the strength in those pictures; the fluid anatomy, klieg-light hatching, the power of that shit, then try to pretend it doesn't intimidate you. And you know, they say some people have a knack for certain things. What I think though, is *certain people* have a knack for *figuring out* things, whatever you give them, because there's a science to everything, a lock with no key, but some cats can go through any door, walk through walls even, because they see that thing not as a locked door but as a process, with simple steps . . . But the way I see it, even in front of a locked door you have to keep churning away, keep moving, you also gotta remind yourself, and that's how I say it, because *I'm no Jim Lee*. What else can you focus on but the time you *do* have, the best you can do, and Sakura, there's things out there you can't even wrap you mind around. And not just Jim Lee! Gil Kane had been drawing comics professionally for more than 20 years, then there in the 70's something in his work exploded. Or Jack Kirby, who I never liked as a kid, the same thing I imagine people have with

Picasso, like the guy was everywhere, everyone always raving about him, and I had to actually get down to drawing every day before I could admit to myself: *OK, yeah, this guy* . . . Or John Buscema! Bob Layton. Joe Kubert. Denys Cowan. Shirow. Mignola. The guy doing those Asterix books. Otomo. Alan Davis. Hugo Pratt— Long list, fade-out; Adam Hughes. Dave Gibbons. BWS. Bart Sears. But that's pre-Crossgen, pre 2000 and who knows what happens to some guys down the line. Ron Lim. Herb Trimpe. Wally Wood . . .

Entropy

Think of your body at rest. You can think about holes, rotting your teeth, your bones becoming brittle, plaque, thickening the walls of your arteries, like that ever-present, ceaseless pressure, building. Or maybe the trick is not to think at all, another eight-hour day, but the surreal part is this fifteen-minute break warming in the sun, convincing yourself it's worth going back. This ice-blue window of time. Your heart beating in your ears, your breath smoking in the cold. Stretched out on the same bench, little park, the fork in the road between 4th avenue and Union Square. The junkies shivering, nodding off around you, birds chirping in bare trees above. Fifteen minutes, with sunlight lancing between buildings to fall across your legs and shoulders, and what you wonder about is what happens to all your big dreams during these weeks at a time when you're just limping along—do they also curdle over, fold up and decay—that's what it feels like, or are they still out there waiting for you, or are dreams themselves part of the churning, infernal machine that grinds people apart, while you sit out here, begging yourself; *Man, wake up . . .*

Art is life: *Pursuance*

To give you my idea of *pursuance*, I can remember for instance, my pal Valdes describing to us the technique of so called "perpetual" masturbation. He'd read an interview, some old porn star, I'm gonna say, Peter North, but don't quote me. This particular bit, the masturbation thing was incidental as it came out by way of a disclaimer that *his* life, the world of a top-tier pornstar was actually more reserved, much more ascetic than one would think. Not only that—and this was the reveal—much like anything, like sports, like Sedoku, that incredible sex stamina was just another microcosmic thing you had to become absolutely consumed with. Because everybody does it, right(?), somehow, some way, but in his case it was about being able to transcend the pleasure, to remain at that threshold, for hours; continually. It got to the point he'd be walking around the house all day masturbating, often stark naked, or at times through the slit in his pants, but casually, watching TV, even on the phone, even all the while during this interview, stroking himself to the point of climax, letting it die down, then back right into it . . . Now this was the sort of tidbit some guys would have filed away for themselves. Instead, Valdes sprinted five blocks from the subway, and that's West-to-East; long, lateral blocks, the magazine rolled in his fist, to the apartment where me and Stasiu lived on 13th street. And from there we should have all become sexual champions, the three of us, which of course didn't happen, though not for trying, though, obviously, what I mean to point out is how this line of thinking could apply to more than fucking girls while working in a bookstore.

Tumescent Guise

BT by the microwave, laughing; some unlikely bit about Haitian dictators, or ancient Rome. Or lecturing me about my sweat glands. But laughing, always with that all-over, itchy laugh, *so whimsical,* and the worst part was I could see him in his own mind like some great raconteur. BT was one of those minefield guys, another one I had to tip-toe around in the warehouse to keep from going into a blinding rage. Not that I'd win a fight with that guy. He was maybe six-four, ugly, big too, missing teeth, and worse, one of those guys, he'd read a few books, and now, mid-life, he'd decided to become poetic. This of course made him a compulsive liar, he was always boring into me with some keenly pitched piece of nonsense, and always topped with some detail that would have me shrieking inside—for instance, the day he met the president, long before the election, before everything. Just two epic men, equal footing, sharing a laugh, having a smoke outside a Chicago office building one afternoon. Who would have thought, yet even then he could feel a kind of, magnetism—And not even the story itself! He'd say this while staring off out the window, into the distance, *as if, what?* Then right away he'd rush to the fountain, you'd have to watch him stand there gulping water in long, theatrical pulls . . .

What else?! Each morning, tying on his little filthy Jamaican do-rag, as if anointing himself with sacred oil . . . This in light of the fact we were all becoming caricatures, half-idiot men toiling year after year in that warehouse. I say this because of my own history of compulsive lying, which no doubt I've mentioned elsewhere. Because it's hard to hate people, that's the thing. I had a girlfriend in college, Elise, and for no real reason, with her I'd lie about everything. My exploits, or whatever, and not even believeable lies, just on and on, while she'd be getting pissed, nearly choking on her food, and I'd be sitting across from her at the kitchen table in her dorm, grinding away, and she'd never say much, barely a word, which is I guess is the way to handle it, to think about that feeling on the inside, reaching and rotting away, and I remember her giving me that withering smile.

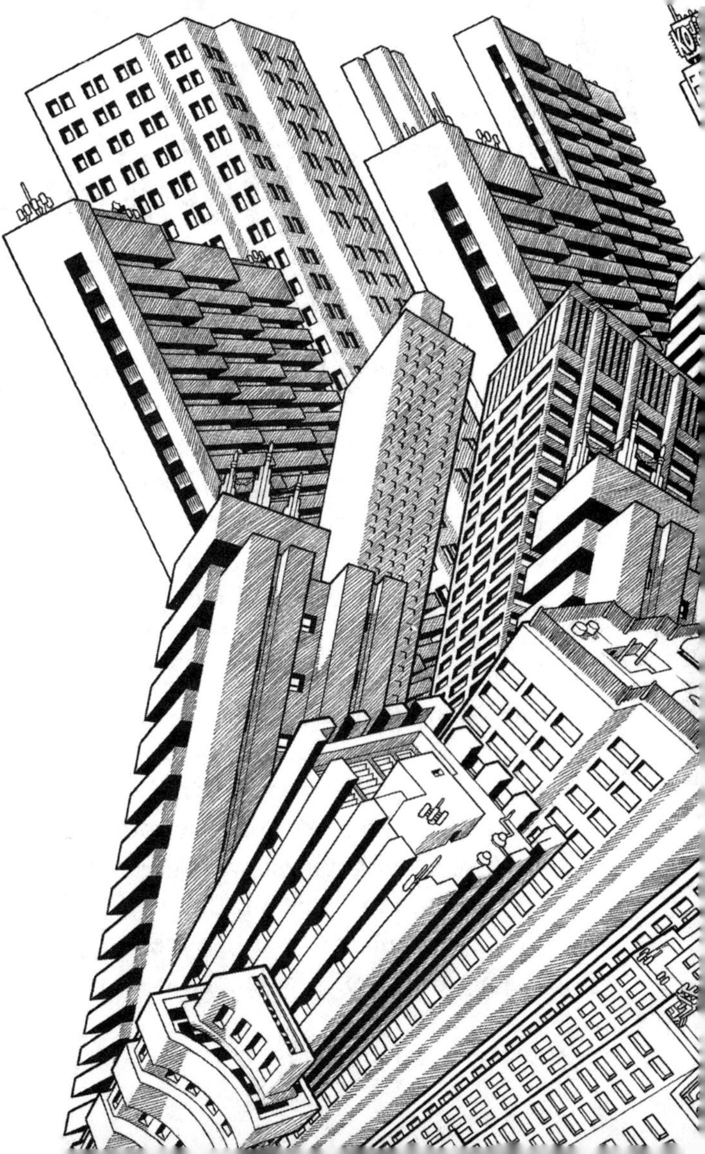

1: Life of Jo-Jo
(Suburbs 1988)

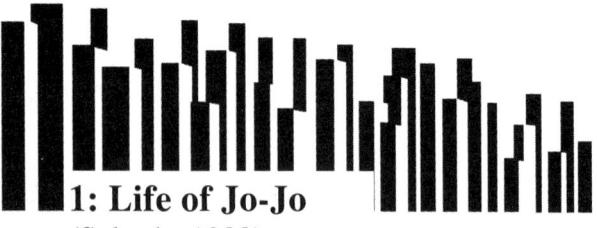

Cloudless skies, the haze off the blacktop. *Man, what else?* Wave and snap. Like five feet of latex tubing, and I'll say we did it so many times I could see the tubes curl, ripple at the ends, the crack that sent those water balloons soaring above the tops of trees, out over the neighborhood for what could have been miles. Also those trees. About the fact of my childhood memory, always the same backdrop, that blurred wall of 20-foot pine. Drop-offs, right from the side of the road, deep into piles of ivy, trees with vines, with green fur that seemed to sweat all summer—and this is the suburbs, not like we live in a jungle. Virgil's neighborhood was rolling slopes, blonde columns. Houses set back from the street. We were the fork, me and Virgil, we let Steve Branham do the balloon, because even back then, age nine, the guy was a linebacker, fucking monster, he'd ease it back until he was squatting on the ground, balloon between his legs, pulling, all three of us trembling, straining, sweating, and that's gay as hell, I know, *on three*, until that whip, *snap,* me and Virgil, torque on the release, like throwing it, then right there in the street, mid-afternoon, laughing, crazy, falling over each other, and the magic was that it was open-ended. For all we knew that balloon smashed a window somewhere, or burst on the head of some asshole on a bible retreat. I'd imagine a picnic, or a carload of dudes we couldn't stand, and if we could get three or four in the air right after the other, then it was a relentless Tokyo strafing run, death from the sky, a love letter for all those jerkoffs, with kids and their parents screaming, skidding through traffic, running aground on the shoulder, the whole neighborhood streaking for cover, and imagining it, just the fumes of that excitement was enough to get you through another week of dead, dull classes, long division in Mrs. Tarber's class, of fifth grade, full effect . . .

The balloon launcher thing. Two, maybe three weeks, bounding around, of hysterical, baboon laughing, teachers glaring at us, then the table at lunch, interrupting each other to further go in on these wild balloon scenarios, also the golf ball, that one time, *man*, like a bullet, *and think about that*. This was the year where the big thing was running up behind girls, early bloomers, getting a good squeeze on their tits, out on the walkway between the gym and the arts building. And not that I hadn't done it a couple of times. But it felt rapey, too savage. Also dodgeball, the new thing in gym class, which was a full-blown war. I was fast enough, but then it was the most I could do to keep from getting creamed. Those sadistic JV football team cats . . . School dances were a joke, one big cattle call, you always left feeling dejected. By then I played so much soccer year-round that my thighs, groin and ass muscles were always sore, which gave me a weird, limping walk that I tried to convert into a pimp sort of pigeon-toe thing, still kind of a bad look.

It was relative, that's what I'd say. For me, it wasn't rebellion. It wasn't about much of anything. Maybe the other roles all seemed taken, the surface of everything paved over and sealed. Or smooth, footfalls on carpet, main hall, 5pm, the cafeteria. Late for soccer practice. That was me, with Virgil, Steve Branham, also the new Indian kid, he had the three empty gallon jugs, that doomped and bumped against his legs as we ran. We circled behind the columns while the janitors worked, to finally slip through, to get two of the little drums of table salt, then out, under the archway, shushing each other, running close to the wall, and in my mind this was the way the world worked, we were the middle-men, the strugglers, but also smoke jumpers, covered in soot, the kids in Oliver Twist. Because no matter what, *something* had to happen. So why wait for it?

2: Life of Jo-Jo

Here's what I'd been waiting for. There were now two Indian kids in our grade, and my main relief was with Bav that seemed to kill off the pressure, the jokes and whatnot, steering me in the direction of Reena Patel. I mean, I was the only black kid, and yeah, she was close, colorwise, I got that part, but she also had a weird, bloated upper body, skinny legs, also that curry-type smell to her, and what, was I supposed to marry that chick? That's Bav, *not Bob*, Roja. To the point where we were saying it too, like that, *Bav, not Bob, Bav not Bob*, because evidently it'd been a thing wherever he'd transferred from; India, or Warner Robbins and it was how he introduced himself, pitch perfect, without fail . . . All of a sudden Bav's following us around, and you know, that's the way. At recess, chopping it up, we're talking, some new plan and there he is, a few steps back, staring at the ground. At the lunch table. Math class, sitting two seats over. At gym, and Steve Brahnam's with the fifth graders, different period, so it's me and Virgil, in line, there's Bav sidling around beside us, and with things like that Virgil's not interested, he doesn't care, so it's up to me to decide how to play it, tricky logic, because in my own mind I'm like a living legend, but then, like Bav, I'm also rail thin with glasses, big head, wardrobe slightly out of touch. And Bav, thin mustache, his polos pressed, always tucked in, always the tight-ass, acid-washed Levis, little guy, but that big-man, bowlegged walk I think is funny, that I guess I like for obvious reasons. Also to bend it back, for instance, the countless times Virgil must have fired that slingshot by himself in the driveway, holding the tubes, stamping the pouch part down and shooting it off with his own foot. First the one he got from Playland Toys, which was nothing, but messing around, taking that apart, to then build the real one with surgical tubing, plastic handles from the hardware store; this is Virgil, C-student, with things like this though, a ringer, a kind of unstoppable, sweaty Copernicus. Meanwhile by comparison, my own ideas felt lame, childish. Fragile's a better word. Also different factors, the map of things you never mention, you don't bring up, standing and smirking, unlikely as it might seem for two guys like me and Virgil, you're there, you're trapped after all, it's either this or be swallowed up, and then, you're pals, just don't think too much about it.

Or forget topography! Or maybe

not rich, not *rich-rich*, only that our North-side, upper-middle, semi-rich neighborhoods all seemed connected, across the river I can't recall even a glimpse of, but rolling, descending and ascending, in station wagons, zooming, in Steve Branham's dad's suburban, curling over and through landscaped hills. Or better yet, the abandoned development in the cul-de-sac behind Steve Branham's house. Like some ruined, unfinished, ancient site. Slab concrete. Thousands of square feet, crumbling, sunk into the hill, sectioned off with staves of rebar and surrounded by a maze of trenches we assumed were for pipes. I thought about that chapter from our history books on the Chinese Qin dynasty, those clay men, rows and rows, sculpted, buried there, posed and marching, like I remembered Mike Shaker, racing his bike off a plywood ramp, leaping to the ground as it went up, out, then down crashing into those pits. Most of the time though, you'd be skirting the edge, top of the dirt wall, fast as you could ride without falling. Or dueling in that maze, sticks for guns, *Double Impact*, diving sideways, or like idiots, running, throwing dirt clods, and not just me and Steve Branham, *Shakes*, also Waddell, Lee James, that crew, Matt Lawson, those guys were wack but they were there, they'd show up in cleats and practice jerseys—this was before, and way up on that hill, through the clearing, from the neighborhood over, every day, that darkskinned kid watching us through the fence. *And yeah*, that must have been Bav.

3: Life of Jo-Jo

Or I'll tell you about Bav's room. The too-tight, tightly made bed. The colors, all grays and beige. Mechanical pencils, desk pad with the calendar, and everything flat, not oppressed, not quite, but checked and counted. Vacuum-sealed, like the dried nectarines he always had for lunch . . . Bav's Star Wars collection, still boxed, locked in the outside closet. I couldn't say why, but I was obsessed, it meant something, and again to those terracotta Chinamen, marching to nowhere. The idea was that even in the afterlife people would still need to be ruled over, *subjectified*, right? So here was this ridiculous, perfect system, as described in our book, a necropolis, preserved under a dome, generals taller than the soldiers, soldiers taller than farmers and so forth, and when they switched off the lights what I imagined were thousands of eyes, from carved, empty sockets, in the dark, glowing.

I said it was relative, sliding scales, and that Friday, the usual, Steve Branham's dad dropping us off, back of the mall parking lot, like, *tell-em' tight, go-squadron*, down, over the hill, and through steam, walking, the four of us, but I can already tell bringing Bav was a mistake.

Blake McCarey. For instance. Blue eyes, he's got blonde hair, the cute perm, but fat in the mid-section and face. Then he goes steady with a seventh-grader, Emily Ogburn, for like a week, not even, just those few days, and automatically the guy's a legend. That's what I was about.

Sliding, fixed fall, rails of an abacus. My secret life. My own room. My drawing table, giant pencils for legs. All that drawing, dead of night, bored, but also probing. Marching, I guess, also thinking, that word, *Necropolis*. We could be cooler, bigger, if I could somehow map it all out.

Down the hallway, Bav's family's apartment. The strange, Hindu knicknacks and baubles on shelves. Carpeted. The smell of curry, spiced food on the stove. Nobody mentions it but since he's barefoot, I'm also padding around, shoes in my hand. We're in his room, which is cleaner, bigger than mine, but with the too-quiet, walled-up feel of a holding cell. Some karate trophies, no dust, polished to shine. He's got a Metroid ripoff character he draws called, Metrocop. Some pretty weak stuff. If anything, I'm more interested in those pencils, the way he draws everything on graph paper, which looks cool, which I've never tried, but he snaps shut the notebook, he goes to the shelf for the Star Wars speeder bike toy and the two figures. He takes down each thing, reverently, almost, but then it's also as if he's holding back. And a weird spot for me, I mean we're all twelve or close enough, we all still have toys but you can feel it, that part's almost over. Not only that but the Star Wars thing's been played out for a while, and these all look brand new. He's putting them on the desk in poses. I come in to pick up the speeder, and he's nervous, I feel his eyes as I take the thing gliding, dipping, digging in because I can see he's afraid, some reason, around the room, lamp in the corner, over the bed, and I'm doing the noise, but real serious, sputtering, buzzing.

Don't get me wrong. If it was a Varnet T-shirt, getting my hair permed, I would've done that. I can even admit I'm sweet on Kate Simmons, but who isn't. Nothing on McCarey, but that guy's a tool, so I'm not deluded, there's gotta be a way to play it.

Friday at the mall I want to call time out, pull Bav aside, but it's a lost cause. He's all over the place, trying to skip coins in the fountain. Or he's by the yogurt stand in some type of Karate stance. Kate Simmons is there in the food court, alive, full-bloom, with like half the cheerleading squad. Meanwhile Virgil still wont say two words to Bav, instead he's talking my ear off, whatever, the Coke machine thing, while Steve Branham's hysterical, laughing, and it's a fog, I barely notice because I'm trudging, eyes to the ground, gritting my teeth.

4:Life of Jo-Jo
(Necropolitan Jump)

Like my dad, Bav's parents were both doctors. So I could imagine him poring over workbooks, long division, some science maybe, but all summer, no TV, at the desk, or Karate, punching air, his dad thinking it was like basketball or soccer, or like the rest of us jumping around in those trenches, which it wasn't, or riding his bike, and I'm guessing it was the yard, the back, the whole driveway, but never, never, not even a millimeter outside the fence, and that's why at the mall Bav was an uncaged, wild moron and why to him girls like Kate Simmons still didn't really exist . . . What my father wasn't, was about five-four with a comb over.

Wooden face. Hard. Those glasses that dark down in the sunlight. Stiff, polyester shirt. Here was the villian, if anything, to my dad's Bruce Wayne and yet he's clapping Bav's dad on the back, easy charm, the usual, bowing, almost, to meet Bav's mother, in fact compared to mine, Bav's parents are both skeletal and tiny, my dad's diplomatic mission, another dinner, and we've been to houses of most of the doctors in town. By this time though, me and Bav aren't even friends. Nothing really, more like a fade out, so we're just there, sunk into the couch, laughter drizzling all around, then later, his room, staring at nothing, then eventually, over and over, listening to the cassette maxi-single, *Party All the Time*, one of *my* favorites too. But I'm distracted. I've still got the cry-baby burn in my cheeks, and before I cleaned up to come to Bav's house, I'd been on my ass, down in that trench.

The beginning was cool. We'd found a burst soccer ball, plastic one, with the yellow insulation stuff inside and it was waterlogged, swollen up, we were punting it back and forth, and because I played soccer I was going for it, elbowing through, I remember I snatched it from Heath Lenington's hands, and I was booming that shit, higher than anybody, we were shoving, chasing it, and out of nowhere, there's Matt Lawson, he grabs me, throws me across the maze, up against the wall. Matt Lawson, he was only the muscle, but then—right—*fucking Pink Persons*, thin-lipped, white goblin, taking his time, and smiling, as always, picking his way, sliding down into the trench . . . Holding the star wars toy, going over and around Bav's room, this is me in my head, replaying the details, and it's like getting my ass kicked all over again. Bav with his storm trooper figure, moving the legs, it occurs to me, though I'm not gonna ask, how much of it he saw, if anything, from his spot up by the fence, but as I'm trying to gauge it the door swings wide, his dad, smirking, and by the sway in his shoulders, clearly drunk. Bav leaps up at attention. I've still got the speeder bike, and from there it's these weird pauses, a surprise for us, *big surprise*, and he's not gonna look my way, only at Bav, smiling, a ring of keys, like some kind of miniaturized pain device, we're padding down the hallway and as I start to wonder if I should be getting scared, there's a closet, he opens the padlock and it's Cloud City, Ewok village, still boxed, brand new, Death Star playset with the carbonite freeze chamber, and vehicles, the B-wing, Millenium Falcon, the AT-AT walker, and stacks and stacks of figures on the shelves, and that's just what I see over his shoulder. The Jawa crawler, I didn't know they even made that thing. I can hear my father laughing from the living room. Bav's dad, drunkenly scanning the shelves, he's thinking, and it could be the fight from before because I'm dazed, one of those hanging, endless moments, me and Bav, and I'm guessing, his first time seeing it as well, or this much of it, floor to ceiling, cardpacks, boxes, and inside, white plastic ships; just the big, Necropolitan idea of all that stuff with light waterfalling, hitting those windows and turrets, splashing around like the inside of a chandelier.

5: Life of Jo-Jo

Hadley Davis. For what it's worth, I can imagine that chick, hours on the phone, lounging on throw pillows in a wall-to-wall room papered in leopard print. She's a cheerleader too, and it's funny to watch her and Kate struggling, talking and laughing, trying to relate. They're always sitting in front, so Blake McCarey's up there too, soft-serving jokes, shooting in their direction . . . We'd only had the two things of salt, three gallon jugs so it maybe hadn't been enough. Also we hadn't mixed it too well, so there was that. The three coke machines in the cafeteria. To get that whole jug down the coin slot, like pumping gas, you had to stand there, listening for footsteps, sweating it out; me, Virgil, Steve Branham, Bav had been the lookout, so I'm waving, telling him, *relax*, but I'm also losing it a little, laughing, water splashing my feet, but that was weeks ago, and now Mrs. Luker's yelling at everyone to sit down, she's getting up to check, opening the door, the hallway buzzing with teachers, custodians, and Sursley, and Blake and John Boston perched up in their desks, craning their necks. Across the room Virgil's nodding, grinning, his idea, because we'd almost even forgotten about it, and there's the bell, lunchtime, we explode through the door, teachers trying to herd us in line, and not just me and Virgil, it's Hadley and Kate Simmons, it's Meg Lyle and Jenny, and David and Mark H. and Mark V., and Jim Terry, it's the whole middle school, buzzing, peering around corners. That's Mr. Lingley on the intercom, crackling, talking around it, but by now we all already know, we don't have to see it, about the machines in the cafeteria going nuts, one of them dead, the other two coughing up drinks; that's cans on the floor, free cokes, spinning, rolling around, those JV dudes falling into a dog pile, and that's better than a snow day, or a bomb going off in math class, that's all those terracotta soldiers climbing out of the trenches and stumbling around. That's Hadley and Blake McCarey asking Virgil what happened. That's me in a pack of cheerleaders laughing my head off, they're sure Mr. Lingley's gonna suspend everyone who took free cokes, and yeah, no doubt, I'm sure too, or whatever, and even though there's no way for anyone to know, I still feel like I'm strutting around under a spotlight. Over with Mr. Neelin's class. There's Bav and his new pack of friends, all wearing their black coats. They seem to hang on his every word, which is funny but also, thinking about it, that's kind of a twist. He's got the collar on the coat flipped up. It takes a second but he sees me, and now it's an easy, slow smile and I'm nodding, *yeah man*, but then again this is sixth grade, after all, week-to-week, so meanwhile there were already other mysteries . . .

Pinkney Henry Persons. Like the weight of those trees, settling, going to night. He gets a running start, shoves me back into the mud, scrambling, I'm soaked. He picks up the ball, spikes me with it, I'm biting down on my lip. Because the last thing I need is to start crying. That time in the trench and who knows, he could've killed me or something, if Steve Branham hadn't jumped down behind me. Steve Branham, who's a monster, who nobody fucks with, us against Pink and his douchebag team, they're laughing, we're faggots and so forth, but they're not gonna make a move, so it's a stand off, my first time seeing him up close, and for weeks after it's his big, smirking head in my nightmares. Something else about that guy, but I can't exactly say. It's October, he's still wearing shorts. Like some stilt-legged, silky bird, and wait, this guy plays football? Pink Persons. Like the two figures Bav's dad gave us. Mine was that guy from the cantina scene with the tumor things in his mouth. Weird villains. Alien creeps. You can fight, that's one way. Or you can try to just move through them, like levels.

No Chop
(Hong Kong 1996)

"Man, thick-
"Thrick." She said
"Big chunks of pork."
"Of pok."
"Like this. With vegetables." I'm grinning, that accent, and she's scowling the words, silver stud, her left nostril, crinkling . . .

"Think I was hallucinating," I said, *"With everyone staring at me. I was drunk too! And hungry! I'm serious. No, listen, I'll make it up to you."*

Hulk Intro Mix

This was me, age eleven or twelve, the suburbs where I'm from, and I can remember something approaching hysteria, walking around the now-pink carpeted basement of the house I'd grown up in. I was in middle school—too young, maybe, a party hosted by a sophomore named Alicia, whose family had moved into the house and was of course, that night, away for the weekend. I can tell you it was like an elaborate prank, played to perfection by these kids, laughing and falling over each other on couches, drinking beer, ignoring me completely as I went from room to room, and it was in that instance, right then, I made the leap to develop a sense of nostalgia.

Fucking white people. And not just the carpet. The track lighting. The vertical blinds, the blond-wood paneling. A phone I saw shaped like a football. The shag carpet cover on the toilet seat, also pink. I remembered riding rings around that basement all night on my big wheel when I was six . . . *All this Sakura*, to tell you about the Suburbs, if you can imagine. I'm not gonna say there was even the illusion of perfection, any more than some great sadness, except for the intro to that Incredible Hulk cartoon. Not the cartoon, but the intro, set to a pounding, orchestral score, and I'd almost dread that music. Same basement, before the carpet. The cartoon itself was an afterthought. I'd sit on the floor, Saturday mornings in front of the television thrilling to that theme and the building idea that life would at some point, speed up, because more than anything, back then, it was the feeling of being stifled, closeted somehow, and it was all like slow motion, like deadsville. I remember that girl Alicia; drunk, big debut, her lipstick smeared across one cheek, like I remembered those screen shots of the Hulk, bursting free from a pile of rocks, wrenching aside walls and tearing out of a prison made of metal spikes. What I don't much recall are the slights, the epic humiliations people talk about, though I'm sure that was there. I can't even recall how I ended up at that party, nor could I tell you what happened to Alicia. Probably married somewhere, with an apron on, and sum of those years for the both of us was a rippling, angry fissure, tearing through golf courses, through tree-lined streets with looping cul-de-sacs, through high school prom dances, through pep rallys, letterman's jackets, through all the changeless, scripted days we felt we had to sleepwalk through—a squeal of tires, a tiny aneurysm at the center of it, that was me at seventeen in the cockpit of my 91' Honda civic, smoking cigarettes, driving around all night, out from that basement into still more smooth paved, gated neighborhoods, soccer practice and orange slices, two day-sleepovers, backyard camp-outs underneath beautiful, ink-black nights and all those white, white houses, blurring by with faux-classical colonnades.

Wendee
(Hong Kong 1996)

Me and Benoit, we discussed this at length. In the afternoons that hung there, floating, curling, out and around like smoke. Those afternoons seemed to drag . . . But the important part was that so far no one felt the need to put rules on us. Whether that was Mr. Leung, I couldn't tell. The Amah. Arms crossed. I'd look up, there she'd be, staring at us. But still nothing. No rules. We could sit in the big room and wait. Surrounded by mirrors. Stare at the girls. We could get out there and beat the pavement all night, handing out cards, working the block. Portland Street, or down in the MTR, those green lights strobing the floor beneath our feet.

Or Wendee. That T-shirt, *Lagerfeld, Fashion Week 93'*, the sleeves cut off, in the afternoons she'd have that over the black dress, or the purple one, on the couch, eating with chopsticks right up until time. Even the idea of her picking that name. And obviously, this wasn't New York, and Wendee, like Thanh, like Khira and Bela, they were all about five and a half feet tall, and dark like Mexicans, it wasn't fashion week either, and what I meant was since there were no rules then why not make what we wanted this to be. In other words, why stand out there circling the block, we could dive, dive for that dream, those parties we watched from the outside, jumping, dive right in, and why think of ourselves as touts or wage slaves, or pimps, I guess, that was Benoit, my thing was the height of it, that deep, shivering dive, and those were the nights you wanted to see every girl, everything, to go on forever, meet everyone. To reach right through . . .

Sosososososo. . .
(Hong Kong 1996)

Wendee. Not that she ever said a word to me. And that name, like some fat secretary. What about Monisha? Khira? In Bangladesh they get black-girl names, according to Benoit. Anyway, 5pm, they're dancing, not even, half-asleep, grinding on each other, Satkhira, that too-plump lower lip, hands on her thighs.

Or Khira . . . The taxi, 3am, now she's wide-awake, haggard, wired. Wedged in, between me and Benoit. And of course that ride from the Wing Wah is like tug of war, but cruising, climbing through clouds, also, more than sex, lights strobing, hungrily, I'll say, across her chest, face, her hand on my arm, pent-up tight, at least until we get to the flat, and she wont speak.

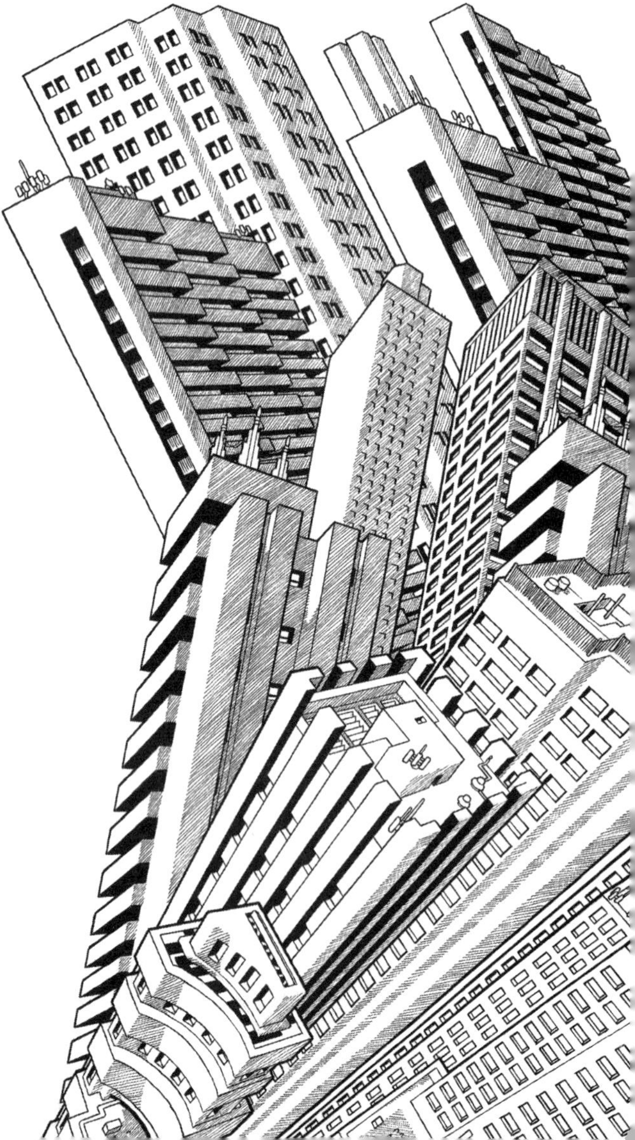

Nothing Works: 1
-New York City 2005

I should be through thinking about it. Ok, but I remember just going batshit, breaking up with Vanessa on the payphone. Hanging up, couple minutes, then I'm bashing the receiver, *bang, bang*, chopping it down, Alphabet City, this two-in-the-afternoon snapshot of my life, that part where I'm always mystified, *and there's gotta be a reason*, like I've been stabbed, because I can't quite believe it, I'm out there fighting the phone booth and staring, at bright red bats, with teeth.

And here again, a single platelet in centrifuge, I find myself spinning, rip-roaring, crazily drawing comics. The hotel room, heat all the way up, so much like those Hong Kong Sundays, sleeping, drawing, afternoons in the stairwell of the Wing Wah, sweltering, soft lull, that gentle respiration, and Sakura, the only difference is another day, another city . . .

If anything, Amy found me through Vanessa. Before Vanessa was everywhere. This was the early days of PDFs, of E-mail, when Vanessa was still going office-to-office with her portfolio to pick up work. Amy was an editor, assistant to something or whoever, but up at the Viacom building in Times Square that was like the grail for those freelance checks, from Nickelodeon, MTV, from Spike, that dotcom, development money. But before that, me and Fabrice were laughing our heads off over her gothic-themed, 200-page short stories; ravens, vials of blood—we were in the MFA program, teaching and writing, or supposedly. Amy was the star-crossed, chubby-faced girl in the class he taught wearing chokers, that bored into him with her eyes, which was hilarious. Until he was sleeping with her.

Of buildings, skyscraping and undulating, leaning-to like palms, waving in a gale. Like I remember Vanessa, that shine of sweat on her shoulders, laughing, pink hair, and those leopard-print jeans. What else? So back to the pad, draw then scratch until pen tears paper. Draw cities while shitting, draw in bed on back, pad in air, line from mercury pen never dry, if not draw then dream, not Vanessa, about men, eight-eyes, with slats in toes, made for concrete, and thin-air thoughts, divining cities miles beneath ground . . .

The Deep Donkey Crew! Sure. The way she explained it, locking onto me with that same gaze. Four-page strip, a webcomic. Based on the Communist-themed, homosexual hip-hop group. Wait . . . *Now, trying to dig into this thing, I'm grasping at straws. Scrolling the jpegs she sent me, pics of these dudes, in speedos, jumping around, and all I can seem to think about are cities. Starting, erasing, wiping my eyes. Time is running out, and meanwhile nothing works.*

Me, Fabrice. And between us, we might've fucked a hundred girls named Amy! Or not that many. While they lived together, briefly, I'd see Amy here and there, campus, or on Broadway, wearing mostly black, and if anything she looked even more tortured, more put upon. I'd stop by and Fabrice too, weirdly, he'd seem as if he'd been crying. On the couch, some sci-fi movie, flickering, paused on the TV. Soon after that, I guess it was over.

In other words, I had to take a second, and I couldn't recall her face, on the phone these years later. Was I still drawing? What was I doing? On the unfinished wood floor in a mess of Tang containers and magazines? *Ah, you know. Surviving* . . . A few days after that phone call, L train, all the way into the city, tapping my foot, I'm licking the backside of my teeth. Pushing through crowds on First Avenue. Get to the place. I see her, at the bar, and a surprise, no more black, except the nice low-cut dress. Her hair is brown now, longer, I'm all instinct, nodding, and yeah, that's funny, about life. She remembered how much I used to talk about comics. Thirty, forty minutes, counting down, so I push right in, kissing, too strong, maybe, but she gives a little, wetly, beer-tinged, before pulling back. *Not yet*, she says, almost laughing. I glance at the floor. She dabs her mouth with a napkin.

"Look, I need an artist. I want to give you some work."

Nothing Works: 2

Or we could make out. Just lie here . . . Which was the sort of thing I'd say to Vanessa, stretched on her couch, waiting, watching her at the table, drawing deep into the night. I'd said plenty of dumb things. *We could crawl all over each other like salamanders, like Egyptian snakes.* Also though, it was quick, from whatever she felt about me, starting off, over weeks, days, I couldn't do much about it, I could definitely feel that dripping, falling apart thing, bit-by-bit, where she stopped listening.

At any rate, grooves in the paper, redrawing faces, eyes, it goes a few laps before you realize you're drawing in circles. Keep moving. Jump to backgrounds. But then each vista, each building is also like a face, little marks, light achieved through halftone, bottom-lit windows, like smiles, and you'd be surprised how much you can f-up a single, ink-puddled check . . . That night in the bar, she gave me three hundred dollars, Amy, cash, the other half after. I had about a month, and I'd be lying if I said I wasn't absolutely certain I was going to knock out this job and then pull off some kind of hook-up as well. On the phone with her for hours, that was the first few weeks. Character studies, turnarounds, drawing these dudes from the pictures she sent me. About growing up, therapy, her distant father, so forth, though after a while I was avoiding her calls. At the time I was in a one-room studio loft, kind of a dump, mid-November, propped under the window with my board, drawing, spiraling, and the real issue with three days left was when the lone radiator sputtered, turned over and died.

But I'm still listening to her voicemails on my phone. Between calling the super. Two more nights. Struggling, trying to think, much less draw, that cold, with everything, chipping at away me. That she remembered how good my stuff was. Bad enough. The tired pinch in her voice. Men always bail on her, I guess. And no, I didn't have to give the money back, to please just show her whatever I've got. Anything. Get back to her when I get the chance . . . But the call I make is to the bookstore, for what's left of my vacation days. Stuffing piles of sketches into a folder, pencils and markers into a dirty ziplock bag. Cut the roof of my mouth trying to floss. *Shit!* I haven't showered in days. On the way out I leave the phone on the futon. No point. And I'm rushing, frantic maybe, but then the one thing I have done consistently, for years, is fail at this. *From there to the hotel. It's funny. Earlier, I figured I'd scout a few places for when I got the chance with Amy. There go those three bones. Third floor, it's a fuckshop, so not even a desk. First thing, I turn the heat, up, up, 80 degrees, with my shirt off, no shoes, I'm already exhausted, fingers of dawn through the window, and as I crawl around on the carpet laying out the different sketches like a map, I realize it's already over.*

My first gig as a freelance artist and, Ok, yeah, this is how it's gonna crash and burn . . . And Sakura, what else do we have to hold on to, dreams and pictures, these easy beginnings to fall back on time and again? Busted, finished, even if it's over, pen to paper, keep drawing, that's what you hear me muttering to myself, sitting against the wall, I can barely hold my eyes open. What would Picasso do, for instance, holed up, dead in the water? What would Gil Kane do? What would Vanessa do, with sketches, photocopies, trickling off the bed, pictures of Singapore, Ankor Wat, what was I even going to do with that stuff? One more about Vanessa, because I'd always fall asleep on the couch, waiting for her to finish drawing. She'd take off her shirt, her bra, get on my back. Breathing. She'd say it right against my ear. "Wake up . . .

Thanh
(Hong Kong 1996)

A glimpse, the window. Through the grate, corridor, other side, the doorway, down the hall in slippers, that's Thanh—I'm not even doing a face, and she bursts out laughing when she sees me. That's back and forth outside for half an hour, pulling myself up by the bars, drop down, running to the next window, same thing, following her on the first floor as she gets the lunch order, walking, strolling around, now barefoot, she brings Mr. Leung his tea, night and day, it was two separate worlds, and the money part was disconnected, vague as the idea of Thanh upstairs sucking dick, mouthwash, all that. One guy I remember;

with glasses, weird little lemur, guys like him, they'd keep coming, consecutive nights, rubbing her legs, pleading for kisses, but begging, that part I didn't get . . .

Those afternoons. Puddles out back, I remember the sky in them, rippling. Pause it right there, but you can't.

She's with Bela, giggling. Kitchen, by the fridge, they throw bits of noodle at me. I'm at the back door. Still laughing, she comes over, no kiss, she puts that 101 Superking filter cigarette right through the gate into my mouth.

The Suburbs

Hyperbolic, starving nights, but that was later. And before you're born into the world there's that silence; nothing, or was there feeling, or better yet, were there cities before suburbs? And no doubt there's theories about it, and books, none of which include early 90's R&B—Silk, Jodeci, mash it up, that out of control wailing, like a sextronic, electrical labyrinth, that is, row after endless row of mini-malls, Taco Bells and Karate schools, empty parking lots end over end, and that's where I looked to the sky to ask the big questions, with my childhood buddy Virgil, eating doughnuts, sprawled on the asphalt beside our bikes, and before you're born you gotta float, dream inside a womb. That hidden fortress.

Two-man Weave
(Hong Kong 1996)

Mr. zero-gee, fade-up. What it seemed like, or that's how it felt to me— *Jump-stop, go back. Some Joe-wobble, man, punch it, night-speed blur, spin moves, shivers.* That's Fa Yuen, off Nathan Road. Not the Lost World, since we both know Nemo, and over there we skip the line. Then again it's a fished-out lake, *no chop*. Find a bar, club. You dive right in. Forget about the Lost World. You tip the bouncer, that's the move, then, full-press. Drunk, backpedaling, the stumble, he recovers, that's part of it. And that's Benoit. He's gonna blow through the door, hi-fiving everyone, or whatever, loud-talking, you think, *this guy's re-*

ally holding court, he's plopping down at tables, but keep in mind he's buying drinks, toasting, he's asking questions, swimmingly, like somersaults, zig-zag circle around the room, and he's gonna pass right in front of our new friends; big, booming laugh in their faces, and that's not a cue, not really. But you tip the bouncer because he's seen this go down a dozen times or more, back to back, night after night. And my part's more of a soft slide. Benoit, he's gonna check his watch, glance over, that's the cue, then I come off the wall, that couple of girls within shouting distance, they're gonna blow me off. I could fall in love, forget it, they might not even speak English, so long as they're smiling, laughing, there's the set up.

For these three guys. Americans. From Canada, maybe, with their polo shirts. With Benoit, flip it, we go in like hawks, real serious, and my part, I try and hold that moment across the table, two-count, say nothing. Take out the card, numbers down, gold side up. *Let me tell you fellas a secret about Chinese girls . . .*

Tostones

Back then I was all about a girl, Kate Simmons. Her pink jean jacket I'm sure I've mentioned elsewhere. My inner life, a blur. I'd started soccer at age four, with my father. When I was eleven I played with adults, with out of shape doctors, lawyers . . .

When I was twelve I played soccer with out of shape doctors and lawyers. Meanwhile my suburb was ablur. Columbians, Jamaicans, tons of African guys. My father is Nigerian.

I was twelve. I gave my heart to Joely Davis. A crunched-up paper valentine, but I was serious. *I like you. Meet me outside after homeroom, the willow tree—shit!*

Meanwhile my father played with

out of shape doctors, lawyers, with middle-aged Africans, Jamaicans. Also college guys, semi-pros. Among them, he was better. Fluid. Sunlight across water. Meanwhile it grew back, but one of my nuts got smashed in a pick-up game with Mexican kids.

I played with adults but I'd be matched against the other kid there, a Mexican, or he was at least Spanish. The tail of hair down his neck that seemed ridiculous. But that was us, *Dos Titans*, and our fathers, what did they think? After twenty minutes his own father would be spent, finished, over on the sideline drinking beer.

And what do you think I dreamed about? Because there was no answer, never, to any of those notes. Sunlight over water, there's a sound to that, but I was serious.

I played soccer with adults, with my father. Meanwhile, in my own separate world with my gang of pals, like soldiers, and on foot we roamed, roved through those neighborhoods that were all connected. St. Andrews. Old Club Road. Steve Branham's back yard, through to the woods. The construction ditch, cut across the golf course, still no answers. The train tracks, the Amaco for snacks. Pineville plaza. Around the back, those two-storey dumpsters . . .

I was deep in love with Emily Ogburn. Call it the problem with riddles, like circles, and the same thing, no answer. It seemed like she was always watching me.

Also Lisa Hutchenson, Beth Watson. Also those Columbians, maybe two families, but with the awning, the stove set up; tables, little kids, toddlers, Hi-fi, the Salsa music, top volume. What else? That shimmering, silvery sound. I'd be on the field, running around, lost in the smell of that food frying.

Satkhira
(Hong Kong 1996)

"Pal, to be honest with you, I don't even fuck with Asian girls like that." He's sipping coffee, saying this. His arm on the bar. This was before they started tearing out the old dais.

"That's real. Yet we're here, surrounded. Besiged. Buried alive, this whole world of Asian girls without asses. Wrap your mind around it. Think about what all this means. Black heroes. That's you, that's me. In exile, from a country that despised us. Stubbed us out. That crushed us, a thousand times over. We were humiliated, spat upon by women. The idea of an artistic life was unthought of, an absolutely-

"No, right. Listen, I think I'm gonna go try and rack out for a couple of hours. I can barely even stand up anymore." I said. Could have been that I was hiding it. Maybe I *was* pissed off, *maybe*, but I was also exhauasted.

But that's what it was like. Suffocating. Purple lights along the ceiling. Third floor, the Wing-Wah, no windows. The mirrors. A maze of mirrors, hallways, and once the image sneaks in, it's over everything, every surface, and when I closed my eyes I could still see Khira rearing back, stretched out on the bed, Benoit gripping deep into the flesh of her waist, fucking and spanking her, and I don't even remember what day it is, night or day, or if I was even sleeping or not . . .

And everybody's got problems! Waking up in the stairwell, rolled in my jacket. Green sequins, throbbing, painful hard-on. Get up, stocking feet, the hallways, into the palace room. And weird without the music, the floodlights, with scaffolding all around. I sat down with the Chinese carpenters, the three of them, in flip-flops, they stopped to give me a once over, then back to chuckling, eating. I lit a cigarette. By now I could tell it wasn't a stage they were building, rather, a wall-to-wall, sectional couch, snaking throughout the room. *Artistic*, if that wasn't exactly the word. Benoit was a megalomanic, that was his deal. My problem was I now spent too much time trying not to think about Khira. With her water gun at the faucet, then up to the light, tracing bubbles in the tubes. Khira, laughing, teaching me the Cantonese words, watching cartoons. Khira. And just about everyone you meet thinks they own you . . .

Canned/Franklin Schneider
(Amazon Book Review)

A down-dirty, grit-covered gem of a book. Mislabeled as humor. Franklin is the pal we all have stories about, like a correspondent on the front lines of a war many of us are afraid to fight. I'd go so far as to say that even if you don't agree with the way he sloughs off society's rules, you've at least wondered about it. You, like me, we've all crunched through pointless jobs, or ones we may even like, and still something's missing. But something's always missing. And this, I'd argue, is what Schneider, would like us to laugh at and understand. Not the evils of culture, or the modern workweek, not necessarily. You can seize up if you want to on the bits about laziness and unemployment checks, but that's the light-hearted, topical fluff. Think about it this way, and it's true; the gifts of the culture we live in were created by thinkers, dreamers, that is, by completely different hands than the ones that use those same dreams to lock us down and enslave us . . . Or maybe that's too far out there. What I like about this guy Franklin though, is there's no real dogma, no ten-step revolution, nor should there be. He wanted off the 9-to-5 treadmill to become a writer, and thus the book, this book, is the proof that we can create the life we want to live, or go down trying. Thus the saga. Sex romps, in unfinished basements. Inter-office pranks. Ten-day benders. The arcade chapter. The dead man in the Porto-Potty. More sex. The sex chapter. More racing, full sprint, down moonlit streets. The lawn mower through the window thing.

This is Franklin's saga. Like we each have our own, and it's up to us to stay awake . . .

Bela
(Hong Kong 1996)

White dudes, these Asian girl experts, and most of them still stomp all over it. I will note, about go-go clubs, you do *absolutely* need a ponytail for this. And I'll say, with Bela, there's a certain type of double-chinned, chain-wearing, Hawaiian shirt-motherfucker—maybe that's the prince she grew up dreaming about . . . And why wouldn't she?

Fortress
(Starring Christopher Lambert)
-Suburbs 1993

Me and Virgil, Nate Elkon. Clouds over the trees and we're gliding, glowing, the usual, driving in convoy, those streets by the Northside highway. Steve Brahnam, he's still fourteen, so he's shotgun, up in front, Virgil's beige Mercedes, like a tank skimming the ground. I've got my arm out the window, sunlight splashing the glass. That's my Honda hatchback, VHS tapes on the seats. That's a line between two points. Like Mr. Paulkiff's geometry class, try to figure it out, or you don't, you either write it off or you delve into it, and while I wasn't big on math I did have those forty minutes from point A to B, between school and soccer practice, twenty-minute drive, but when you break it down that's way more than enough time, pick up Steve Branham, to hit the DQ, Arbys, the backstreets, you gotta stay out in front of Elkon, who drives like he's in some kind of Thunderdome, also that last sprint above the highway, alongside the fence, gun it, the intersection, then there's the mall, deep down there, nestled, and it's that in-between space, circling, weaving in that maze of parked SUV's and pickup trucks, sky already pink at the edges, minutes left, that's a few laughs in the parking lot, a cup of coffee, turn up the music, and that's freedom anyway, hotbox a couple cigarettes, blaze out.

But about the movie *Fortress* . . . To read into it, he's down in this prison miles beneath the earth's surface. At some point, a sex scene, glowy-lens, a dream, he's with a blonde chick, she's riding him, then right as he starts to get into it he's snatched awake by robots and they punish him, they're gonna lobotomize his brain for just daring to think about it.

Jie, Lue
(Hong Kong 1996)

Blocky, big porcelain teeth, chicklets. But then Lue was the type to stare at the floor, mouth closed, and here's a thing I think girls have trouble with, Chinese and otherwise. Because there's different types of pretty. Anyway, Jie did the talking. Jie was also tallish, flat-faced, so she was the one with ideas, loosing them both from those factories in Luoyang, Songxia, from Shenzhen, over land and water, clouds and thunder, all the way to Hong Kong, the Wing-Wah, and now what? Also, weird machines, 3-arms, with flashcards, the assembly-style language schools, the promise of English. If not factories then pimps . . .

Professors. Boyfriends. Formen. If not money then what? Stacks of money, sweeping mythology, more promises, that much I knew about. I didn't speak Mandarin, I was listening though, it was Jie chattering in Lue's ear, scolding her, or some diatribe, back in the corner, or on the couch, but again, off to one side while the rest of us ate, and Jie's got a grip on her arm, smoothing her hair, insisting, whispering, and I'm thinking about Lue in some street level, filthy office, flinching, her real front teeth being pulled out one by one.

If I had to guess, I'd have said Lue's dream was to pile enough money, get back to the village, the town she came from. Open a store, hair salon, maybe. Maybe that's what she told herself. But you gotta frame it. Khira, her little dance, foot to foot, around in a circle. Jie, Lue. Thanh. Bela. All of us. Scottie, the busboy, Chinese kid, the girls ignore him completely, even cruelly, and not just on the clock. But in other places, I've seen the kind of savage way Chinese men handle the girls, *Chinese girls*, mind you, and these are games we play within ourselves. Jie and Lue were the only two actual Chinese girls at the Wing Wah back then, that was important. And Lue, with her mouth closed, was a statue; milk-white skin, flat chest, a museum piece, and I'll say, I couldn't imagine her fucking. Eight times out of ten, guys go with Khira, any of the other girls, and I could tell Jie thought Lue wasn't trying hard enough. My thing with Lue was to somehow get them both out there with us on the street. To think about Scottie, also that always-there cluster of local guys out front, looming, looking and staring. Now take that same show on the road. For the expatriate set. That's me and Benoit. Sequined jackets, forking down noodles, so forth, but we're out there with two smooth, tall Chinese girls, and it's about Lue, the breeze in her hair, that face, and forget handing out the cards, she's not gonna smile and I'm not even gonna try and convince you, but see us around Mong Kok, strolling, lounging, in and out from that doorway off Nelson street with the purple lights, and it seems to be open all night.

The Deuce
(New York City 2010)

I blew off Jackie, I told her, forget about the coupons . . . Two-for-one dinner-date, Brooklyn, select restaurants, twenty-eight bucks, and what's that gonna buy me? Forget the first hour, which is easy. That could be testing out pens, looking for my ruler. It could be putting on socks, on then off again, too hot, or stretching, still not drawing, at the table, my chair, against the springs, I'm tense but I'm bouncing. Right outside the door, there's Zhanna—again, in the hallway throwing that ball, and singing, and now she's really drilling it against the wall. Jackie's on the phone. Real loud, she's stomping around, crashing dishes in the sink. Turning on the fucking blender. I get it. *And Jackie, if not this then it's sitting in some restaurant clearing our throats, treading water, you say there's nothing to talk about anymore, but from my view what I'm doing is watching life swirl down the drain while we're talking, talking about loan payments and new furniture, and sitters, and school fees, about why we need a car, about five years down the line, about Zhanna, she needs a sibling by the way, a brother, about whose turn it is to do the dishes and it's two hours, Jackie, give me that much, let me concentrate, and whatever it is I'll co-sign it, go out on a limb, we'll say, forever, that extra beat, if we could bite down and skip over some of this talking . . .*

Then that second hour. Trying to imagine a soundproof room. I could do the walls with egg cartons, those black foam stalactites. I could get another room, a hotel. A new girl, maybe, I could forget it, start over. But that quiet is a prison, and it's one way or another. That's with or without Zhanna outside the door singing pop songs. While I'm sealed off, iced out on the couch, or curled up, dreaming, or staring at nothing, the stub of my blue pencil, I'm trying, and it's not waiting, more like I've got to hit rock bottom each time, draw the same thing in disgust, over and over then finally, time's almost up, and of course now the stops are out, *that's what I'm doing in here, Jackie*, and it's like that vacation we took, the Holiday Inn downtown. Sunshine through the blinds. I'm flying, drawing. Fight-free. Rolling.

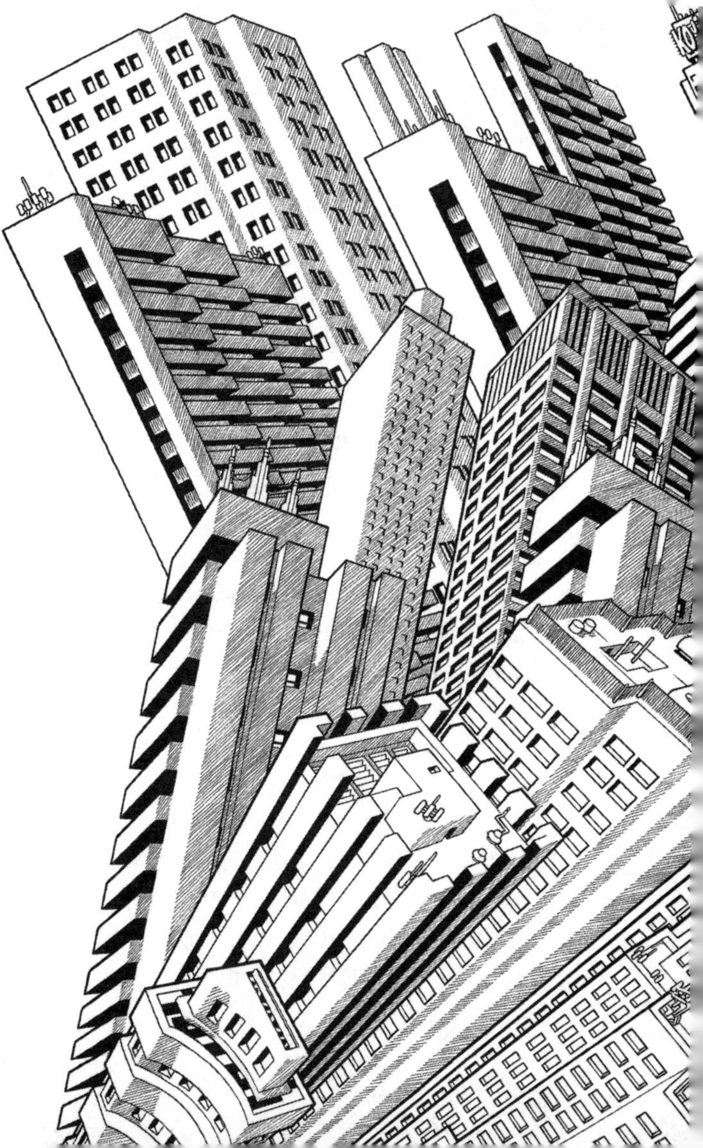

Monisha
-Hong Kong 1996

She's dancing, *dancing*, keep in mind. Fluttering, *yeah*, jogging hips. Hand all down the crotch of her bathing suit, Khira, ridiculous, that's trembling, shimmering thighs, like sliced meat slick with sweat, and glitter, she's got you, from the mirrors, and not just her; hundreds, a thousand Khiras . . . I'd wake up, bathroom, or on up to the roof landing to relieve myself. Jerking off in the stairwell of a go-go club. *That's heroism!* That's purple neon, the bright, bright whites of her eyes. Forget Khira. Half-empty beer, down it, find a cigarette. We've got the jackets on, doors open at seven. That's lights-up, hit the streets, for me and Benoit, not *cold,* cold, but smooth . . .

And we'll be talking, whatever, movies, about Henry Miller, that night, the Prince versus Michael thing—arguing, just walking, *yo, get loose*, over sidewalks, medians, and some girl, dyed auburn hair, maybe I'd seen her before, but on into the crush of bodies swarming Portland street. Two guys; tight jeans, bewildered, grinning, and we can tell, their first few days in Hong Kong. Benoit jukes right past, pushing between them. They stare at the sequins in his coat, smirks on their faces, that's the hustle, and I come on up, I throw my arms across their shoulders . . .

By eleven o'clock we've roped maybe three guys back to the Wing Wah. Slow night. We're chasing too much, forcing it, so we pit off into Blush. The girls there know us, swimming up with big smiles, which helps, to a point, I'm back-to-back with Benoit, he's working some old guy, forties, with two Filipina girls, edge of the dance floor, and now I'm gulping drinks, I've got the card, thumb and middle finger, the music, doing that little chop with my other hand, and it is a kind of dance, the spiel, not so much talking as reading eyes—cut-back, now switch it so I'm talking to the girl, try that, she's listening, laughing about it, he's with her for the night, but he's looking at the card too. *Yep, listen, I want you to fall in love*. I shout, leaning in. *But not here . . .*

"By the way, this shithole?" and that's Benoit, zero to sixty, *"And you've never been to the Wing Wah? Blue! Yo, Blue! Look at this fucking guy. Woww, man, two girls? You know, it's a good thing you bumped into us!"*

Wait. Ok, Monisha. Holding my face, scratchy, silver stud in her nose, the mouthwash taste on her lips, and like she's reaching, blindly grasping at something, her eyes pressed shut. From there to that afternoon. Palace room, lights down. Crouched against the wall, I'm smoking, and there's Monisha, between doors, rushing, tears, split-second, and her chin, trembling . . . At any rate, 3 am, and we've bailed, given up completely. We roll in right as Khira gets back, that's *fast food,* I've stopped trying not to think about what that means. She's fucked another couple of guys. That there's a few hours left though, before morning, and she wants barbeque. Clapping her hands about it. Round up a few of the girls. I grab Monisha. But on the street the whole thing sours on me. Loose, getting flaky. Quick pull from Benoit's flask. Or three, or four. Jumping, everyone's laughing. Khira's all on Benoit, kissing his neck, arm around his waist, she won't even look my way, and tonight, it's hard to stomach. And Monisha, trying to walk next to me.

We should hold hands, maybe, but I'm stumbling, looking at lights. Vaguely aware I'm now on my knees, of people staring. Crawling on the sidewalk, I'm searching. Drifting. That girl with the auburn hair. Who of course, doesn't exist . . . *But I am Monisha!* Rather, trying to picture her back in Jhalokati, in Dhaka, or wherever. *Like busting through paper-thin walls!* Three months ago I was in college in Iowa City. Now barbeque, siu mei. Coconut shavings. Benoit, with his lover-man face, nuzzling Khira. Drop an ice cube in. That same cup of coffee over and over. Sip it. Then back to the microwave, hit it again.

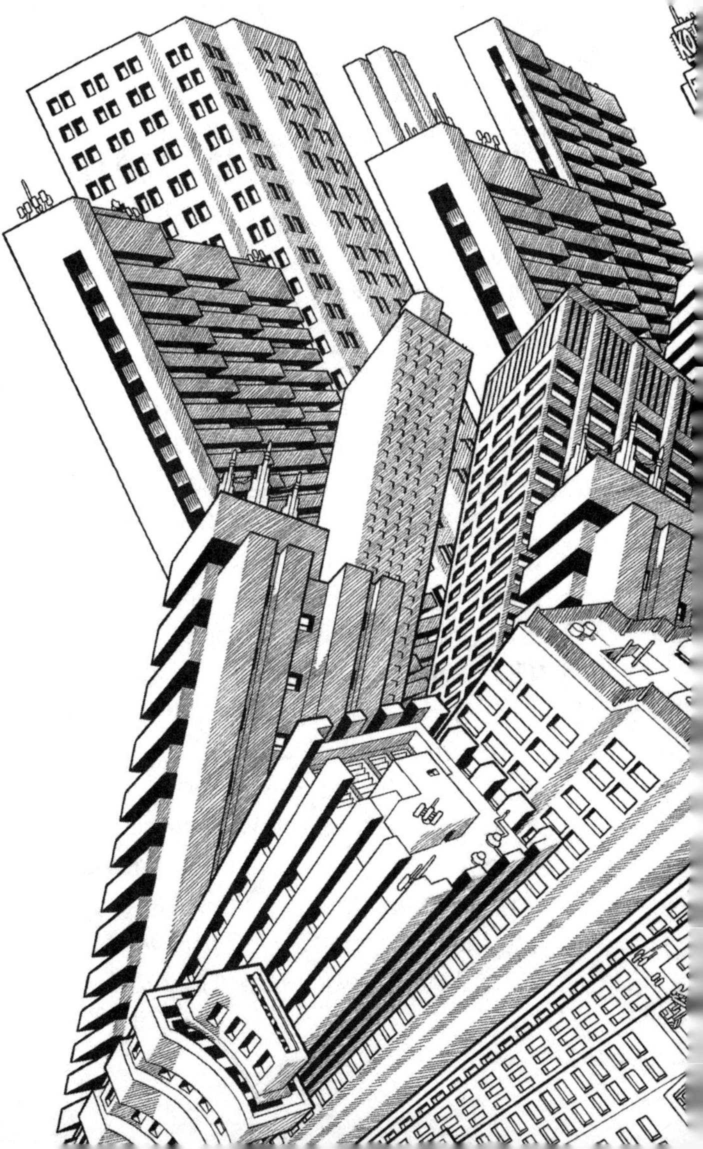

1: Cumulo-Nimbus Tonight!
(Hong Kong 1995)
-Friday December 31st 2:20 AM

Not just for dear life. Squeezing that bar, swinging on the outside of the railing. A little scream, scrabbling with my feet against the side of the building, flakes of rust digging into my palms. Funny how moments like this are pure sensation. Puke on my breath. The sweat in the armpits of my silk shirt. My asshole, puckering. I'm in fact, sweating bullets, and I feel, more than I really see the deserted, rock-hard sidewalk way down below. Even in the moment I can admit how lame it would be die this way, and I can imagine the postscript: *Unknown American falls eleven stories to his death. Girls at party remain unenthused.* Unknown because I'd left my passport, phone cards and money in my other jacket, back in my room at the YMCA, which had been only the beginning of a bad night . . . And not that I was the most charismatic guy! I was no big champ, but it was almost unreal how this day had spiraled downhill and it was also funny how quickly you start to lose faith in yourself. First in the cab, those girls peppering me with questions, then losing interest, then stampeding with talk right through whatever I'd think to say. *Man, all that giggling.* All that racing around, down Bonham Road, from Wan Chai, the Mid-Levels, to Central then back again. Racing to meet other girls, all of them squealing and hugging each other while me and Dustin stood off to the side like two jerks. Most of those other girls couldn't even remember Dustin, didn't seem recognize him at all and this was the guy who was supposed to be my ticket. Like flailing, slipping down some dark hole. That girl Doris. Chinese Doris, with daggers, and of course she catches me looking in the rear-view of the cab, pouting and smearing scented lip-gloss around her mouth with the little wand. Standing in that café with Dustin and those girls, with Doris and her white friend, sipping iced chai tea while they talked about friendship beads and the other stuff they were all about in high school. More than that though, I'd been off my game for weeks. Like I was some weird, scorched leper, talking to girls. Some hooded pervert, cackling and limping around, at the Lost World, at bars, while everything I tried to say felt like a stumble.

But no, what I was holding onto, I guess, struggling with, was the idea there was still some point to this. I'd dropped out of school over a month ago in Iowa City. Booked a flight from an ad in the newspaper, *Experience Hong Kong*. An impulse move, but also a thing I'd jumped into with the idea of a grand purpose. I was gonna draw comics. But when I said that to people it didn't sound big enough. Aside from the fact I could barely draw! So I was going to teach myself, forget Iowa, but smack in the middle of a city that made me think about comics, that moved like comics, where the real action took place. Arriving in Hong Kong the first night though, I found I couldn't exactly say what that "real action" was, and from there even the few art supplies I needed turned into a saga. Even when I left the hotel to buy soap, or a hot meal, this too would usually mean the beginning of some weird, spiraling adventure, and from there it was stepping outdoors, like zooming down, dropping through feathered clouds into those streets like canals, teeming with phosphorescent life. Exhausted by day then fumbling through vivid, wide-awake nights, including, but not limited to this thing on the balcony, that is, arriving in Hong Kong, skip the preliminaries, fast-forward right to me easing out that tiny window from the bathroom with shaking hands, sick, dizzily pushing the grate aside, gaping at the eleven-story drop then heaving myself across the gap, the two or three feet to scramble over the balcony railing and flop, gasping, onto the patio, lying on my back with sounds from the party inside nestling softly over me like a breeze.

2: Cumulo-Nimbus Tonight!
(Hong Kong 1995)
-Friday December 31st 12:40 AM

"Okay—but wait. Get what I'm saying."

"What are you saying?" Now she was annoyed. *"Dude, you're rambling. And it's no big deal. I get it. You're comparing comics to a language. You're trying to make it sound so complicated."*

"Jill, I don't mean to seem too smug. I don't know, let me say it another way." But I was backpedaling, also shivering, on the couch, and swaddled, the sequined green jacket thrown across my shoulders like a blanket. Which *was* kind of ludicrous. But also the way she was trying to write me off.

"Look. Whatever. You stay on your little mission over here, with your disco jacket, I'm gonna go-

"Hold on. Hey. Relax. And let's say—complicated—only in the sense these things can sometimes get that way. Right, Jill? Give me that much, and look, I'll admit, yeah, I want to impress you. I mean, I wasn't actually thinking about this stuff when I left Iowa, but here's what it's turned into. And it's not a comparison. Comics is a language. I couldn't teach a class on it, any more than I speak Chinese, but if I had a blackboard, we could break down three or four simple shapes, much like the few basic sounds that we can all make with our mouths. And that's no matter what language you're gonna speak. If you get me. And hold on, hold off before you rip me up. It's different because you said you've been speaking Chinese since you were five. Right? Cantonese, whatever. You're

not Chinese, but you might as well be. So it doesn't seem complicated. You conjugate verbs, use different tenses, long chains of vocabulary, but think about the path of that process. And back to those shapes I mentioned. With drawing you've got, let's say, the sphere or ball, the cube, and the cylinder. I could tell you those three shapes comprise everything, but it's only simple once you don't have to think about it. Think of words not as tools, but vessels. A sound with the same shape for everyone, but what do you fill it with? Ludicrous, I know, and like I said, not to be smug about it. But Jill, that's a formless maze, years, and hours, and you've got to start at the very beginning and wade your way through."

A formless maze . . . Like a sweat-soaked towel tied round my head. Like talking, moving underwater, my stomach and bowels churning, bubbling—while she sat there glaring at me, and I could barely hold myself upright. There were ten or twelve other dudes, at least, besides me and Dustin, mostly white, a couple of Chinese cats, but like prep-school guys from a catalogue, all dressed nearly alike, laughing, opening beers and chattering, bouncing, milling around Doris and the other one, the other hyper-caffinated Chinese girl I was never introduced to, but both of them like turbines, driving this thing, flirting, laughing hysterically, about whatever, little spurts of dancing, for no one in particular, but all of us watching, and if there was any music it was drowned out by the shackled-down roar of the situation, *think about it*, look but don't look, that same old pressure as always, building . . . On the other hand, Jill was supposed to be best friends with Doris, and who knows what the deal was with that. Chinese Doris, the lycra skirt she had to keep tugging on, and all night she'd been preoccupied, with the phone in the kitchen, dialing then hanging up, then waiting, dialing then waiting. Every so often one of those guys would come over, maybe try rubbing her arms or a hand on the small of her back. This is what Jill was really watching while I was blathering about comics. They were friends, I suppose the way me and Dustin were pals, but I was also ticked off, about done with that guy, perched on the edge of the couch, a full beer in his hand, and holding it like a tricorder, talking to no one; flat, dull, barely trying, but sitting there as if to decipher from it some lost algorithmic code.

3: Cumulo-Nimbus Tonight!
(Hong Kong 1995)
-Friday December 31st 1:50 AM

Also that shirt! And from the beginning, meeting up with Doris and Jill, I guess knew the kind of night this was gonna be. Doris, in spike heels, strutting around, laughing too loud, and then Jill, uneasy about it, crossing, uncrossing her arms, but still in that skin tight, cap-sleeved t-shirt, **Hong Kong**, with those huge D-cup jets busting right through the logo, a kind of glitch-hop, post-post-disco MTV Asia, and there *must* have been music going because I'm following that other Chinese girl with my eyes, she's still dancing, jogging a circuit through the tiny living room, around the couch, the table littered with half-full plastic cups, whipping her hair around, weaving between bodies, and this bit of open-air swimming, watching her is enough to finally get me off the couch, down the hall to the bathroom where I throw up immediately, and neatly, into the toilet . . . *For instance, this girl dancing. You start with the torso. Through-line with a curve to it. Forget the details, you draw the gesture, long swoosh, two stretched cubes, rectangles, the arms—cylinders; loose, floating, her head a thrown back sphere, and so on* . . . Throw up then I sit, shitting, and it's all liquid, spraying the inside of the bowl. I light a cigarette. I'm trying to filter back through the whole conversation, layers of bullshit, layers and layers, and me drawing in the air with my finger—*was I doing that?*—and those glitterpuff letters buckling, stretched across her chest, everything loose and distorted, the sequined jacket—thankfully I wasn't wearing it now, and if there was anything at all, anything sincere about comics I could go back out and say to her, then I was reaching for it, fumbling in the dark . . . *It wasn't the Alcohol! And why was I even talking about it? With her!* Now I'd become that guy, art-prick at the party, playing that card, because I'd been trying to claw my way into the game all night. Those girls hadn't seen Dustin since high school. Not only was that our ticket, it was also his big chance to reinvent himself. Which had been my pep-talk, and somewhere in the scheme I'd also assumed I'd be able to get into conversation and loosen things up. Or not. Or rather, I'd spend the evening as dead weight, me and Dustin, trudging behind those girls while they laughed amongst themselves, stop after stop for Doris to use the pay phone, and maybe even a moment in the beginning, they were asking about Iowa City, but there also I fumbled around too much with words, withering under pressure, and that girl Jill seemed to really enjoy watching me choke out in slow motion . . . *Also think how much of human interaction is a kind of shell game, about subtext. Again, start with the torso, frame beneath the frame. You imagine the movement of what you can't see . . .*

All this back and forth, and in the midst of it a deep welling up within me. Reflex, my jaw locks open, I double over and throw up on the floor between my feet. Panting, dry-heaving. I sit there for a minute, staring at the mess before the situation starts to seep in. I stand up and wipe, using the last few sheets on the roll, hit the flush, which shudders then dies off, leaving the bowl full of puke and shit. *You gotta be kidding me.* Panic. Standing now, pants around my ankles. My mind racing, quickly doing the math. Everyone was in the living room and kitchen, which was set off from the bathroom by the hallway. It wasn't as if I could walk out and ask for a plunger. Or a mop. *Because I took a huge dump that won't go down, and by the way, I also puked all over your bathroom!* Then again I couldn't just waltz out like nothing. Or could I? The living room led out to a balcony. And if I remembered right the balcony was only a little more than arms length from the bathroom window . . .

SupaMillenialNight-Speed-Falcon
(Hong Kong 1996)

I think about that night and imagine myself running. Better yet, a running, veering, wildly sprinting, nameless silhouette inside of a logo, going, running like crazy, and inside of that—not stars but lights— a flower bursting open, the city itself, Hong Kong, jump to hyperdrive, boom through streets. And those stars stretch out . . .

Smash-cut to me falling through clouds—or, seemingly, right through clouds, into a couple of garbage cans, *on Rodgers street*, that part I remember, and everybody's laughing; those girls, even Dustin, and it's off, into traffic, horns blaring, I'm zigzagging, stumbling, those few beers, and I'm sweating, this weird fever, then again all that's just an excuse. Then later, dry-heaving, crouched in the gutter. This must have been after that party, and we never did meet up with Nemo, we stood in line outside the Lost World for as long as I could stomach it, and Dustin was still there behind me, and as usual he'd wait this one out. *And what about that party?!* Or skip out to the end. Zooming around, turning without brakes, and because I'm drunk the idea is to soften me up, the old cross-harbour tunnel thing. Pulled over, there on the shoulder, bathed in the lights of the two cabs, and it's not just my driver, the Kowloon taxi guy too, he's pissed, also a third guy, Hawaiian shirt, interpreting, *and wait, where's Dustin?!* And they could sack me, take my money, that's the funny part, instead we're negotiating; smiling, interrupting each other, I've got the sequined jacket over my head like a turban, *and fellas, who else is blazing through these nights? Listen, forget the money. Not only are we like brothers out here, we're strugglers, we move man, we're on a mission . . .*

4: Cumulo-Nimbus Tonight!
(Hong Kong 1995)
 -Friday December 31st 1:26 AM

"Yeah, no. But you're saying-

"You're being too melodramatic, that's what-

"Hold on." I said, *"If I was one of your pals, talking about law school or something you know you'd-*

"I'd what? Agree the plan would be to move to another country? Self-teach yourself to become a lawyer?"

"Right. Ok. I'm-"

"In a sparkly, tuxedo jacket? Would I?"

"Ok, I'm a douchebag."

"I didn't say that."

Thrashing, twisting around, struggling. She was looking right past me, into the kitchen, and here I was invested, straining for something, if I could pull her back, as if it mattered, and the loose, chunky feeling in my stomach wasn't helping . . .

Then also, over there, the cloud of guys floating, waiting around Doris, who was still hovering by the phone on the countertop, still playing it cool, or trying to, and meanwhile there'd been a pecking order established. White kid, the piercing in his lower lip, with the triple-wide, neoprene skater pants, easing her away from the counter. He was moving in, soothing her and she's playing along, over-laughing, draping herself on his shoulder, a high-five he makes sure to end with clasped hands; *nice move*, I guess, though she's acting like she's strung out on something.

"*. . . like a language, with comics, with drawing, it's just like that, you could spend years in a classroom, wasting time.*" Glitch-hop, fade in and that's me, still talking, and Jill's rolling her eyes.

"What do you mean, wasting time? Dude, I had a Cantonese tutor when I moved here. It's not some magic you pick up roaming the streets."

"Isn't it? Think about-"

"And stop telling me what to think about. Do you try to game everyone like this?"

Blurt—pause, short lapse, chasm, she's looking around. I wanted to do something, smash a bottle, anything; to jump right up, out of my skin, whatever, something drastic . . . The other Chinese girl, now she was off in the corner, by herself, whippng her hair, dancing with abandon, and crazily, sloshing her drink on the floor. With that roomful of dudes, movie extras, milling around, or glued to the wall, watching. The whole thing, verging over. If I could wake up, gather myself. *Focus. If this bitch would crack a smile at least, if I could move her with something!* In fact, *not if*, no question, I was about to set this thing off, *T-minus, control the party, lets do this*, that is, if I could just get upright on the couch, untangle myself from my jacket. If I could somehow settle my stomach — and *uh-oh*, here comes smooth Chinese bro across the room, smiling . . .

"Lei cumman du tong n-go gong yet la?" she said, and that's what it sounded like, all vowels, and they're in a little stand-off, smiling at each other, until the guy lets up, laughing cheesily, then it's in for the kiss on the cheek.

"Go-geen jacket. Ogoo lei mm-jon-geela, hi mai?" she said, then after a beat, *"This is Blue. He's into comic books."* Ouch.

"Hey," I said, taking the handshake.

"Hey man. Tony. You're a friend of Dustin's? Cool, man, cool jack-

et. Yeah, that's Josh over there." He points to the guy in the skate pants wrapped up with Doris, who's also laughing cheesily, hysterically, as the guy salutes us with his middle finger from across the room.

"He's joking. And hey, sorry the place is so bare, we just moved in, like two days ago. The only thing we've bought so far is the stereo and this couch."

The couch, beer in cups, the skate pants. I glanced around the smallish, suburban-style apartment, which I assumed in Hong Kong must take a fortune to rent. Not that I was expecting an opium den, or whatever, but we could as well have been in Iowa City. And this guy with his claw-spiked hair, the chain around his neck and basketball shoes.

"Dusty. Long time, man. By the way, where's your brother?"

"Passed out somewhere, proba-

bly." Snorted Jill.

"*So, yeah.*" He said, nodding. Long gulp of beer. *"For New Year's. You guys doing Lost World tonight, or what?"*

5: Cumulo-Nimbus Tonight!
(Hong Kong 1995)
 -Friday December 31st 2:30 AM

On the concrete, blinking, *the balcony . . . Right*. Stand up and I feel brittle, spinning inside, so I stay there with my back to the party holding the rail, call it meditation, that hot-night cityscape glowing from below, and I can pick out not words but voices, and not to existentialize it, the sound of people's mouths wide open, roaring, ludicrous, and maybe that's what I'm into, moreso than parties, the gearing up for it, and I'm already piecing together in my head another little cute sermon for Jill . . . *Hey, hi. It's me.* On the other hand, what was she so skeptical about? I try to remember what conversations at parties were supposed to sound like, to ignore my stomach, which was still churning uncomfortably. I imagine myself a wounded soldier, returning to throw myself into battle—or rather, returning the long way, staggering through that endless, illusory maze, echoing with laughter, pulling a sac of my own angrily bubbling entrails.

Rather, back to the party, *ease into it*, my shirt now soaked with sweat. I stop at the door to roll down my sleeves, button the cuffs. Walk into the room and right away I notice Jill hawking me over some guy's shoulder. Did she see me on the balcony? Could I get her number? What's that look? And Dustin. *This guy*, like a concierge, standing at the edge of a group, middle of the room, his cup of beer keeping him afloat. Yeah, I could imagine him in high school with these cats. And my thing was, you had to fight your way in, somehow, some way, fuck the rules, and some guys never would, all that bottled-up ache . . . Big, drunken smile on my face as I swim in the thick of it, laughing, pressing palms, clapping dudes on the back. Talking at the top of my lungs. A sort-of sideways glide, moving towards Jill, *look but don't look*, and meanwhile the tension had ebbed, drained from the room and what was left was a kind of pause, disbelief. *Keep moving*. Over by the counter, this guy Josh trying to get Doris to drink a glass of water, there's another guy with him, also a ton of gel in his hair and the looks of concern on their faces is almost too much. Doris on the phone again, dialing, the strained look on her face. I get to Jill, still with whatshisname, with Tony, she's laughing, talking into her beer like it's a microphone, and before I have a chance to go too far a loud smack wakes us all up. Back to Doris, the cordless handset, she's shocked as the rest of us, staring at it as if waiting for some answer, then she rears back and bangs it again against the counter, then back again for another one before Josh and his buddy swoop in, *whoa, whoa* . . .

"*Whoa.*" I say, and Jill's there next to me, incredulous, but Tony's rushing over. A few other dudes also, all night they've been statues but now's their chance. Like linebackers they've got Doris wrapped up, cradling her, holding her by the waist. Someone's got a towel under running water in the sink. They've taken the phone from her, but wait, now she's snatched it back. She's brawling now, flailing around, and of a sudden all the attention's too much. Bracelets ringing, fighting free and now what? She's at a loss. She wants to dance again, stumbling to the middle of the room and now there's definitely no music. The sound of her five-inch heels scratching the floor, she's still holding the phone. *Not yet*, but I'm already going for my jacket. Dustin, his beer, hand in his pocket, saying nothing, along with everyone else watching Doris in freefall. *Buddy, soak it in*. Another huge crash. Across the room, that other Chinese girl on the floor, out cold, the same team running over, clustered, kneeling around her, now someone's heading to get this or that from the bathroom(!) and, *whoa, buddy, time to go, my stomach's killing me and plus, those chicks were off on that apocalyptic-nimbus-cloud-old-testament-ish . . .*

Space is the Place
(Hong Kong 1996)

There's the moment. Jump into it, and this is after that party, after I missed New Year's altogether, that crazy fever or stomach flu, whatever it was, and here's the inevitable crash, a week later, the flat feeling, the arcade, for hours, messing around with that soccer game.

"So what, you stalking me?" she said, and there's a smile to it. *"What are you doing here?"*

And not Fifa, its Sega soccer; faceless polygons and those sluggish controls, the pitch racing, pulling beneath you; drop down, cruyff-turn, that army of defenders in a crashing wave, falling, sliding all around, blowing you up off the ball, into space. And not that I was so into it . . .

"Doris." She said, laughing, ticking off a second finger. "The thing with the phone. And that other chick."

"The way her head smacked on the floor. Oh."

"And you didn't even really see it. She was gone. Out cold."

I'd been there all day, for days, my back up straight, chain smoking, eating those shrink-wrapped croissants from the vending machine. And coffee. And the rotating clique of INT kids by the front, leaning and posing with their sunglasses on. Smoldering. Clowning around. Bear hugs and lit cigarettes, laughter all around, like I said, it's been days, coming in first thing in the afternoon, and I guess I am technically, actually stalking her, and wait there's Jill, *man, look casual*, that tightness in my chest and this is after seven or eight nights of me dreaming about kissing her up against the wall on some 80's movie tip, this is watching her walk toward me down the aisle of consoles, scales on a vibraphone, like jazz in Tunisia, blonde hair in her eyes, no makeup, and those pink, pillow-soft, white-girl's lips.

"I dunno. We got off on the wrong foot. Maybe I was hoping for another chance."

"A chance for you to what? Shit up my bathroom and puke all over the place?"

"Let's skip over that. Or, I mean, I'm fuzzy on the details. Besides, if I can tell you something, Jill, I'd never, never shit up your bathroom."

"You're wooing me with that?"

"Let me tell you something else. All week I've been stuck on that tight t-shirt you were wearing-

"Get over it."

"But wait. Powder blue. Shit! Those puffy letters. I love Hong Kong, can I say that much?"

6: Cumulo-Nimbus Tonight!
(Hong Kong 1995)
 -Friday December 30th 7:03 PM

To give you an idea, Nemo was always hunched over, leaning on something, smoking. Awake but squinting. Tall, but slouching. Same damp grey T-shirt, flipped inside out, untucked, or the brown one, but the hair was the thing. His hair was a kung-fu wig, dyed chestnut, blown back into spikes, and it was funny to imagine him throwing on dirty clothes, then spending an hour carefully pulling his hair with gel into those dozens of little points. The blurry tattoo of a swooping bird with the one wing going onto his neck. And how could you explain it? Keep in mind that almost without exception you'd hear these girls laughing about him as a loser, dismissing it, but after a while you'd know what's what. After a while you realize he's fucked all of them, their friends too, or would eventually, and between guys that magic is space exploration, like tectonic plates, an incredible frontier. And not just any girls. You could pretend it was the same, that it didn't matter, but these were girls you dreamed about for months after, they made your chest hurt, Chinese girls with milk-white, shimmering skin, shades in the daytime, in velour, in silk shirts with epaulets, girls with soft, ultraviolet smiles, laughing, stalking behind the ropes in front of the Lost World club, where Nemo was a busboy, and in a way to see him and Dustin side by side, as brothers, it made sense, that weird calm, the same uninflected presence, one side flat, the other freighted and alive, with something. With electric nights. That ticklish, oscillating, warp-speed wonder, because you wonder about it, out the back way, punching through rear doors onto the street outside Lost World, that one night, one of many, and this guy's got yet another unbelievable girl leaned into a phone kiosk, skirt hiked to her thighs, and he's in there, not even kissing her, just posing, both hands holding her face, and that line of spit on her cheek and I remember the way she looked, like complete surrender, mesmerized . . .

Dial that back, way back, reset, move a muscle, and it was the way all those nights began. From blues to black, and almost dark as we hit the street, the alley behind the McDonalds where I worked off the books. Fire at the horizon, glowing between buildings. Ethereal light. Purples and pinks. Neon Dragons, flickering to life . . . Nemo's teal truck, blinkers, door open, parked at the mouth of the alley. The clack-clash of spoons against those giant woks from the open back doors of the food stalls. And the thrill is like a third lung opening in my chest, *get after it, do anything*, and I'm putting on that jacket in super-cool slo-mo, half-turn, my fingers grazing the cuffs, the green, glittering sequins, and I'm clapping my hands Flamenco-style, no reason. Dustin, looking at the sky. Nemo wincing, checking his beeper, unlit cigarette behind his ear.

"Yeh, man. Crazy. That stuff turns up in the box every week. Yo, Jackets. Watches. Shoes sometimes." He gave me a once-over with the sequins. *"But you like that? Got a few more in the truck. Like a leather one, some kind of-*

"Nah, it's good." I said. "It's perfect. Don't know if I can pull it off though. We'll see. But listen, with these girls tonight, what's the plan?"

And on cue, his beeper erupts again angrily, buzzing, trembling on his belt.

"Man, these INT school girls. This one, back in ninth grade she was a duckling, but now she's hot, and she don't know what to do with herself. Yo, she's been buzzing me non-stop since this morning." A snort, pointing at Dustin, who just stands there, his slight smile. *"Anyway, he knows, they were in the same grade together. They were little pen pals, trading poems and shit, for years. Like I said, she's alright, some cute friends, whatever, but I can't get that whole crew into the club tomorrow. Fuck that. Fuck those kids."*

"Whoa, wait, poetry?" I said, turning to Dustin. *"Like sonnets and shit? Let's talk about that for a second . . .*

Acknowledgements

To E. Ellen, also Aaron Burch (Hobart!). Thank you for taking a chance on this ish . . .

Shout to Nathan Tower (*Bartleby Snopes*). Roxane Gay (*Pank*). Andrew Lipstein (*Thckjam*), *Black Heart Magazine, Boston Literary, The Newer York, Adroit Journal*, Justis Mills, (*First Stop Fiction*), Carissa Halston, (*Apt. Magazine*). Sorry for "shotgunning" you.

Shout to my pal Bill Ham, to Macon Georgia. Abbey Sparrow, Stu Pickett, big boy Josh Branham, to Russ Jacobs, RIP. To Rachael, for reading all those crazy letters. Shout to my pal Frank Schneider. Same saga. Mike Valdes. *Just keep writing. Whatever else you do.* Patrick Koisewicz. Leonard Ko. Taylor Segrest. Sean Genell. (*All The Help You Need*). Brandon Graham (*King City, Prophet*). For drawing comics with me in the Strand breakroom. Patrick Eamonn (*Fresh Green Beast*). Isaiah Ensua-Mensah. Greg Farrell. Maud Pryor.

To my folks, Dad, my Mom, don't give up on me. And to Ford.

Ijeoma.

I'm gonna keep trying to keep trying to thank you. Thanks forever.

About the Author

Uzodinma Okehi spent 2 years handing out zines on the subway. *Wasn't as fun as he thought*. His work has appeared in *Pank, Hobart, Bartleby Snopes*, and many, many other places, no doubt, you've never heard of. He has an MFA in writing from New York University. He lives in Brooklyn. His son is 8 yrs old, smiles a lot, (too much?), and will absolutely, cross you over and drain a jumper in your face.